"WHAT DO YOU WANT?" KEENA MOANED. "WHAT ARE YOU TRYING TO DO?"

"Maybe I'm trying to get you to stop running from me," Nicholas said thoughtfully.

"But I've never run from you," she protested.

He searched her face with slow, darkening eyes. "Honey, you've done little else since the day we met. You'll let me get just so close before you start backing away."

"Do I?"

"What are you afraid of, Keena? Is sex such an ordeal for you that you've given it up, or are you afraid that I'd be rough with you? You do seem to have a knack for making my temper boil, but believe me, I'm not an impatient lover."

"I'm not afraid of you like that," she replied. "Just don't rush me, Nicholas."

"Rush you, for God's sake!" he ground out, his dark eyes blazing. "It's been six years!"

A WAITING GAME

Diana Blayne

A DELL BOOK

Published by
Dell Publishing
a division of
Bantam Doubleday Dell Publishing Group, Inc.
666 Fifth Avenue
New York, New York 10103

ISBN: 0-440-21066-6

Printed in the United States of America

Published simultaneously in Canada

August 1991

10 9 8 7 6 5 4 3 2 1

RAD

To Mary and Georgia, with love

January 22, 1991

It is my great pleasure to see *A Waiting Game*, my very first Dell Candlelight Ecstasy Romance, back in print again. I worked for a textile manufacturing company as a girl, and I learned a lot about the business from just watching and asking questions. There are no more wonderful people in the world than those who work in textiles. I still have friends and relatives in that field.

In the original plot of *A Waiting Game*, two things were changed. First, Keena started out inexperienced. I make no secret of my preference for innocent heroines, but an editor I respected asked for an experienced heroine in this book. Also, originally Keena was a redhead, which was why Nicholas called her, affectionately, "little fox." I loved Nicholas from the very beginning—he was a big, lovely man with a loving heart and a wounded spirit. I still claim him as one of my favorite heroes.

I hope you enjoy reading this book as much as I enjoyed writing it. I still enjoy the part about Nicholas and the painter, after all these years. *A Waiting Game* was a real joy to write.

My best to all of you.
Love,

Diana Blayne

One

Keena Whitman's day had gone backward from the moment she got out of bed. Two of her best sketches had been destroyed when Faye turned a cup of hot coffee over on them. Naturally, the sample-room staff had been livid when they had to wait for Keena to redo the sketches so that they could make up the rush samples for the salesman. Like all salesmen, he was impatient and made no attempt to disguise his annoyance. She'd missed her lunch, the seamstresses had missed theirs, and

1

to top it all off, she'd gotten the specifications wrong on a whole cut of blouses, and they had had to be redone with the buyers incensed at the hold-up. By the time Keena was through for the day and back home in her Manhattan apartment, she was smoldering.

She kicked off her high-heeled shoes and threw herself down on the long, plush, blue velvet couch with a heavy sigh. How long ago it seemed that she'd worked at textile design and dreamed of someday working for a big fashion design house. And now she had her own house and was one of the most famous designers of casual wear in the country. But the pleasure she should have been feeling simply wasn't there. Something was missing from her life. Something vital. But she didn't even know what. Perhaps it was just the winter weather making her morose. She longed for the freedom and warmth of spring to get her blood flowing again.

She lay on her back and stared at the ceiling. She was slender with short black hair and eyes as green as spring leaves. Her complexion was peachy, her mouth as perfect as a bow. At twenty-seven, she retained the fresh look of innocence, despite her sophistication. At least Nicholas said she did.

Nicholas. She closed her eyes and smiled.

A WAITING GAME

How long ago had it been when Nicholas Coleman had offered her the chance to work as an assistant designer in his textile empire? It was well over six years ago.

She'd been utterly green at twenty-one. Fresh out of fashion design school in Atlanta and afraid of the big, dark man behind the desk of Coleman Textiles in his Atlanta skyscraper.

It had taken her a week to get up enough nerve to approach him, but she'd been told that he was receptive to new talent, and that he was a sucker for stray animals and stray people.

Even now she could remember how frightened she'd been, looking across the massive desk at that broad leonine face that looked as if it had never smiled.

"Well, show me what you can do, honey," he'd dared with a cynical smile. "I don't bite."

She'd spread her drawings out on the glass surface of the cluttered desk, her hands trembling, and watched for his reaction. But nothing had shown in his dark face, nor in his dark brown, deep-set eyes. He'd nodded, but that was all. Then he'd leaned back in his swivel chair and stared at her.

"Training?" he'd shot at her.

"The—the fashion design school, here in

3

town," she'd managed to get out. "I . . . that
is, I worked on the third shift at the cotton
mill to pay my way through. My father works
for a textile mill back home—"

"Where is back home?" he interrupted.

"Ashton," she replied.

He nodded, and waited for her to continue,
giving every impression of being interested in
her muddled speech.

"So I know a little about it," she murmured.
"And I've always wanted to design things. Oh,
Mr. Coleman, I know I can do it if someone
will just give me the chance. I know I can."
Her eyes lit up and she put her whole heart
and all her youthful enthusiasm into her
words. "I realize there's a lot of competition
for design jobs, but if you'll give me a chance,
I promise I won't let you down. I'll design the
sharpest clothes for the lowest cost you've ever
seen. I'll work weekends and holidays, I'll—"

"One month," he said, cutting into her sentence. He leaned forward and pinned her with
his level gaze. "That's how much time you've
got to prove to me that you can stand the
pace." He threw out a salary that staggered
her, and then dismissed her with a curt gesture and went back to his paperwork.

He'd been married then, but his wife of ten
years had died shortly thereafter of a massive

4

heart attack. Rumors had flown all over the main plant, where Keena worked, but she ignored them. She didn't believe that an argument had provoked the heart attack, and she told one of the women so. Mr. Coleman, she assured her tersely, wasn't that kind of man. He had too much compassion and, besides, why would he keep a picture of his wife on his desk if he didn't love her?

Somehow the innocent little speech had gotten back to him and the next week, he'd sought her out in the canteen on the pretense of asking how everything was going.

"I'm well on my way to making you fabulously wealthy," she assured him with an impish grin as she held her plastic coffee cup between her hands.

"I'm *already* fabulously wealthy," he replied.

She sighed. "In that case, you're in a lot of trouble."

He'd smiled at that—the first time she'd seen him smile since his wife's death. The late Mrs. Coleman had been a beauty—blond and delicate, a perfect foil for his size and darkness. Since her death he'd been strangely lost, and his temper had become legendary. He spent more time at the plant than at his office, and threw himself into the accumulation of other plants to complement it. His holdings and his

5

wealth had mushroomed in the months between, and the pressure was telling on him. His hair was growing silver at the temples; his eyes were boasting dark shadows. His tireless business dealings were becoming the talk of the plant. Mr. Coleman was out to become a billionaire, some said. Mr. Coleman was after a business rival, others said. Mr. Coleman was going to make his empire the biggest in America, if he lived, others commented. But only Keena seemed to see through the relentless businessman to the lonely, grief-stricken man underneath. The other employees might think Mr. Coleman was indestructible, but Keena was certain that he wasn't. She would run into him occasionally in the elevator or in the cafeteria. She recalled one time in particular when his eyes had seemed to seek her out. With his coffee in hand, he strolled over to her table and sat down beside Keena and her friend Margaret as naturally and easily as if the three met for a coffee break every day.

"How's it going, Miss Future Famous Designer?" he asked Keena with an amused glance.

Keena had laughed and given him a flip reply, something about an interview in *Women's Wear Daily*, hadn't he seen it? Margaret finished her coffee and excused herself quickly.

"Did I say something I shouldn't have?" Nicholas asked, staring after the young woman.

"The company brass makes most employees want to run for cover," Keena explained in a dry tone.

"You aren't running," he observed.

"Ah, yes," she agreed. "But then, I've never had much sense."

He chuckled into his coffee, taking a long sip of it. "The patternmakers sing your praises, by the way. They told me your specs were the first they'd had in five years that were written in English."

"High praise, indeed, and I hope I'm going to get a ten thousand dollar a year raise as an inducement to keep them in a good mood?" she grinned.

"Cheeky, aren't you?" he asked with narrowed eyes.

"It's my dimple," she replied in all seriousness.

He shook his head in mock despair. "Incorrigible."

She looked at him—so businesslike and somber in the vested gray business suit that strained against his massive, muscular frame —and dropped her eyes almost at once.

After that day he'd made a point of having

7

coffee with her once in a while. Infrequently, he'd invited her out for a meal, and they'd talk a great deal. She'd asked him once if he had any family, and he'd replied stiffly that what there was of it wasn't to his liking.

"It still hurts, doesn't it?" she had asked quietly then.

He stared at her, his face closed up. "I beg your pardon?"

She met his eyes with compassion and utter fearlessness. "You miss her."

He seemed to see right into her mind in the long minute that followed, and the hauteur slowly drained out of him.

"I miss her like hell," he admitted finally and with a faint, fleeting smile. "She was the loveliest creature I ever knew, inside and out. Generous to a fault, shy." He sighed heavily, his face darkening. "Some women can tear a man down with every word. But Misty made me feel every inch a man every time she looked at me. We married because it was necessary to keep the businesses in the family. But we grew to love each other desperately." He glanced at her. "Yes, I miss her."

She smiled at him. "You were lucky."

He scowled. "Lucky?"

"Some people go through life without ever touching or being touched emotionally by another human being. To love and be loved in return must be magic," she finished gently. "And you had that for ten years."

His eyes had searched hers before they fell. "I never thought of it that way," he said simply.

"Shouldn't you?" Her voice had been gentle and low. And while he was still thinking about it, she changed the subject completely, telling him about some ridiculous mix-up that had occurred in the cutting room that afternoon.

It was sad that he and Misty hadn't been able to have children, she had always thought. They would have made him less lonely. But she could see that he seemed to find solace in her company, and they had worlds of things in common, from a mutual love of ballet and the theater to classical music and art. She found in him a mentor as much as a friend, a tutor, and a protector. Nicholas never made a pass at her himself and was fiercely protective. He scrutinized the few suitors she had over the years and gave her his advice, welcome or not, on the men she went out with. If she had to work late, he escorted her home himself. And when he felt that she was ready, he'd found her a job as an apprentice designer in one of New York's grandest fashion houses. He'd encouraged her, pushed her, bullied and chided her until she climbed straight to the top, which was quite a climb for the only child of a poor, widowed textile worker in the small Georgia town of Ashton. She didn't like to remember her childhood at all. In fact, Nicholas was the only person she'd ever told about it. But then, Nicholas was like no one else. In a real sense he was the only true friend she'd ever had since she left Ashton. And shortly after she'd come to New York, she was relieved to know that Nicholas maintained an apartment in the city.

The phone rang, and she barely heard it, so deeply was she immersed in memory. She was used to Mandy getting the phone, making coffee, serving meals, but this was Mandy's day off, and it took her five rings to realize it. She dragged herself to the end table and picked up the receiver.

"Hello?" she murmured, stifling a yawn.

"That kind of day, was it?" came a deeply amused voice from the other end of the line. "Get on something pretty and I'll treat you to dinner at The Palace." She felt her spirits revive. "Oh, Nicholas, we haven't gone there in months! And they make the most marvelous chocolate mousse."

"Can you make it in half an hour?" he asked impatiently. "I've got to catch the eleven o'clock plane to Paris, and we won't have much time."

"Has anyone ever told you that people who don't slow down get ulcers?" she asked, exasperated.

"They would have to catch up with me first," he told her. "Half an hour."

She stared at the dead receiver. "Nicholas is an enigma," she muttered as she slipped into a long green velvet gown with a deep V neckline and a side slit. He was every inch the high-powered executive, and he had millions, but he wouldn't delegate any responsibilities. If a deal had to be closed, he'd close it. If there was a labor relations problem at one of his plants, he'd negotiate it. If there was an innovative process being presented, he'd go to see it. He pushed himself relentlessly even now, a habit left over from those first horrible weeks after Misty's death. He wouldn't slow down; he wouldn't take time off. It was as if he were afraid to stop, because if he did, he'd have to think and that wouldn't please him. He had too much that he wanted to forget.

Keena was dressed and waiting when the doorbell rang. She opened the door and mentally caught her breath at the sight of Nicholas in evening clothes, as she always did. With his dark hair and eyes, his bronzed complexion in that leonine face, his towering, wrestler's physique, he was the stuff of which feminine dreams were made. And perhaps if Keena hadn't been so wary of men, so unforgetting of that humiliating adolescent romance and the humiliating incident that had followed it, she might have fallen head over heels in love with him. But she'd seen Nicholas in action, and she knew the effect his dark charm had on women. She'd seen his occasional conquest swoon, fall, succumb, and be heartlessly discarded too many times to risk joining that queue herself. Nicholas had found safety in numbers since Misty's death, and he was apparently risking no emotional involvement by confining himself to one woman. Keena preferred the position of being just Nicholas's friend and confidante. It was much safer than being added to the notches on his bedpost.

His own eyes were busy, sliding up and down her body with his usual careless appraisal.

"Delightful," he said with a cool smile. "Shall we go?"

"I'm starved," she told him as they got into the empty elevator and Nicholas pressed the main floor button. "I feel as if I haven't eaten for days."

"You look it too," he growled, eyeing her

12

from his lounging position against the rail. "Why the hell don't you give up that diet and put some meat on your bones?"

"Look who's talking!" She glared. "It would take a forklift to get you up a hill!"

He moved toward her with a dark look in his eyes under that jutting brow. "Think it's fat, do you?" he taunted. He caught her hands and dragged them to his shoulders. "Feel. Show me any flab."

It was like discovering fine wine where she had expected to taste water. She'd never noticed just how broad Nicholas's chest and shoulders really were, or how the scent of tobacco and expensive cologne clung to him. She'd never noticed how chiseled his mouth was, or how exciting it could be to look into his dark eyes at close range. It had been safer not to notice. But her hands touched him through the smooth fabric of his evening jacket and lingered there when she felt the hard muscles under it.

"Well?" he asked, a strange huskiness in his deep voice as he looked down at her.

"You . . . I never realized how strong you were," she stammered. She looked up into his eyes and time seemed to stand still for a space of seconds while they looked at each other, discovering facial features, textures, expressions in an unfamiliar intimacy, in the quiet confines of the elevator.

It took several seconds for them to realize that the elevator had stopped and the door had opened. Self-conscious and a little clumsy, Keena managed to get out a little ahead of him and lead the way to the front of the building where his white Rolls-Royce waited with Jimson at the wheel, staring straight ahead stoically.

"Doesn't Jimson ever get a day off?" she asked Nicholas when they were inside the car with the glass partition up, giving them total privacy.

"Not lately. I've been working twenty-five-hour days," he replied.

"I'll never get used to this car," she sighed, leaning her dark head contentedly back against the leather as he was doing.

"What's wrong with it?" he asked curtly.

"Nothing! It's just that few people ever get to ride around in a Rolls—white no less," she laughed.

He half-turned in the seat, one big arm over the back of it, his eyes gleaming, though his smile had not completely disappeared. "And what's wrong with that?" he asked with deliberate slowness.

She braved his glittering eyes. Why did he

look so suddenly predatory to her? So dark and menacing? "Nothing—except that I feel as if I were on display every time I ride in it. That's all."

"You should be on display, Keena." Something in the way he fairly growled her name sent a warm, unfamiliar tingle up her spine.

"Because I'm rich and famous now, you mean, and everyone back in Ashton would hardly recognize *this* Keena Whitman?" She laughed shortly, her words underscored with a note of self-derision.

Her answer hadn't pleased him. It was in the hard lines of his face, the narrowing of his eyes. "No, not at all, though you needn't take that little-Miss-Nobody-from-Ashton tone with me. You know what you are and what you've accomplished. And that you're a very beautiful woman," he said in that hard, matter-of-fact way of his.

If he had been looking at her, then he would have seen the shock register on every feature. Keena was suddenly thankful for the darkness between them and the sudden blare of a horn that had broken Nicholas's steady gaze for just that instant.

"Damn city traffic," he muttered half to himself. When he turned back to her, it was with a faintly puzzled expression. "Surely you've had

15

men tell you that before, that you're beautiful? Scores of them, I'm afraid." His words broke off abruptly, his gaze dropping to her slender body, outlining it with a masculine approval that was new and frightening.

"Why are you looking at me like that?" she asked in a faint whisper.

His dark quiet eyes eased back up to meet hers. "I was wondering what it would feel like to make love to you."

Two

Her toes tingled. She'd never felt such a wild surge of emotion and it came up suddenly, stunning her.

Nicholas began to chuckle, the deep sound of it faintly irritating.

"My God, what an expression," he murmured, leaning back against the seat with a heavy sigh. "I thought that would get your attention."

She glared at him. "Now that you've got it,

what are you going to do with it?" she asked grumpily.

He glanced at her. "Get you back to the present. I loathe self-pity. Wait until I'm in Paris. I've got enough problems of my own without your dragging new ones from the past."

"What kind of problems?" she probed.

His lips compressed. "Maria."

Maria was his mistress. Keena had read about the relationship in the gossip columns long before Nicholas had introduced the two of them. It shouldn't have bothered her. He was, at forty, an active, virile man, and it would have been absurd to expect him not to have women. But one evening soon after he'd picked up the volatile brunette, Keena had seen them together in a popular night spot dancing so close that the fabric between them seemed to burn. And she'd begged her escort, a harmless young man who'd only lasted one date, to take her home. She couldn't bear the sight. She'd hated the surge of jealousy, but it had persisted until even now she could hardly bear to hear Maria's name.

"What's wrong?" she asked, trying to sound casual.

"She won't believe it's over," he said curtly. "She's calling me in tears twice a day, moaning over the lonely life I've condemned her to.

18

Lonely, my foot, with two diamond necklaces, a new Porsche, and an ermine coat!"

"Maybe she really does miss you," she muttered, able to be generous now that she knew he'd lost interest. She felt strangely relieved.

"She misses the Rolls, honey, not me," he laughed shortly.

"Was it good in bed?" she asked, tongue in cheek, and darted a glance at him.

"The Rolls or me?" he replied, refusing to be ruffled.

"I imagine she misses the warmth," she retorted, grinning at him.

His dark eyes smiled at her. "Do you think I'd be warm?"

"Like a blast furnace, I'd imagine," she said demurely. "Is that why you're going to Paris, to escape Maria?"

"It isn't funny," he said, the smile fading.

"No, I don't suppose it is, to you." She shot him a teasing glance. "But your love life is like one ongoing adventure to me. I really think you should assign the girls numbers or something so you can keep things in order."

"I'm delighted that my private life amuses you so," he said in a chilling voice.

"You could always tease me about mine," she said grandly.

His dark eyes cut around toward her. "You

19

don't have one," he said, "not a love life anyway."

Her eyebrows shot up. "What makes you so sure?"

"I keep a sharp eye on you, little one," he said with a somber tone that startled her. "Sharper than you know. You don't sleep around."

She glared at him. "Maybe I should hire a private detective of my own!"

"What do you want to know?" he asked with a wicked grin. "Go ahead, ask me. I'll tell you."

She glared at him again. "I'd just love to ask you something so personal it would embarrass you to the roots of your hair."

"Dream on, honey," he returned with a smile.

She sized up his muscular, imposing physique. "I'll bet you crush them," she murmured absently.

He lifted an eyebrow. "Is there only one position?" he asked in all innocence.

The blush started at her hairline, worked down into her cheeks, seeped into her throat and down into the plunging neckline of her dress. And he sat there and watched her and laughed softly, lazily, as if the sight delighted him.

"Instead of the theater, I'd better start taking

you to some X-rated movies," he murmured. "Your education is sadly lacking."

She opened her mouth to speak, but before she could manage a retort, he picked up her hand and pressed her palm to his lips. It was unexpected, and the sensation it caused made her heart turn over wildly. He caught her eyes, holding them in the dim confines of the car until she felt as if she'd never get her breath again.

He drew her forearm against his lips, sliding it past his rough cheek, holding her eyes the whole time, studying her like some rare and beautiful thing he'd captured.

"I use my elbows," he whispered, drawing her imperceptibly closer, his voice caressing, seductive. "And I've never had a single complaint. Would you like me to prove it?"

Her heart was hammering wildly in her trembling body. She stared at him and couldn't look away, and she was suddenly afraid.

"Little coward," he murmured, watching the expressions chase each other in her eyes. "Are you really afraid of me?"

She cleared her throat. "I'm hungry," she lied.

"For me?" he asked humorously.

She tore her hand out of his grasp and

edged back into the corner by the door, glaring at him like some fierce little animal.

"You're priceless," he chuckled. "Did you think I was going to make a pass at you in front of Jimson?"

"Jimson is trained not to look," she reminded him, her voice strangely breathless. "And it's not kind of you to make fun of me."

"I can't help it; you rise to the bait so sweetly." He cocked his head at her, his eyes watchful. "Haven't you ever wondered in all these years what kind of lover I'd be?"

She averted her eyes then dropped them. "Yes," she said finally, because she'd never made a habit of lying to him.

"Well," he prodded. "What did you think?"

She glanced at him with unfamiliar shyness. "That you'd be heavy," she grinned.

He laughed softly. "And what else?" he persisted.

She shrugged. "Tender," she said softly. Her eyes met his across the space. "Patient. A little rough."

"Not demanding?" he asked quietly, and there were deep undercurrents in the conversation.

"Are you?" she asked involuntarily.

"It depends on the woman," he replied. "But

I can be patient. And tender, when I need to be."

"How . . . how do you like a woman to be?" she asked breathlessly.

He stared at her, his eyes darkening, his face hardening with emotion, and there was an electricity between them like nothing Keena had ever experienced.

"The Palace, sir," Jimson's pleasant voice interrupted their wordless communication as he stopped the car in front of the exclusive restaurant.

Keena drew in a breath in relief, wondering what had gotten into her to make her ask such an intimate question. *It must be my age,* she thought wildly, waiting for him to come around and open her door.

"I think we're going to have to do some talking when I come back from Paris," he said on the way inside. "I've got something in mind that might benefit us both."

"You want me to design you a wardrobe!" she said with mock enthusiasm. "Something suitably flashy, but elegant, to go with this car. Frankly, I don't think the job's for me, but . . ."

"Damn you!" He burst out laughing in spite of himself. "Come on and feed me before I take a bite out of you!"

It was impossible not to notice as they made short work of filet mignon and lobster, buttery rolls, a salad, and rich red wine that he was paying more attention to Keena than he was to the food.

She stopped in the act of lifting a piece of steak to her mouth, staring across the white linen-covered table at him. "Why are you watching me so closely?" she asked with a faint laugh. "Afraid I'm going to try to walk out with the silver?"

"You remind me of a pixie," he murmured absently. "Mischievous little face, teasing eyes slanted just a bit at the corners, perfect little mouth. You look as if you're out of place in this setting, and I've only just noticed it."

"I'm twenty-seven," she reminded him, "and I'd hardly fit under a leaf in somebody's forest."

"Twenty-seven," he echoed quietly. His dark eyes narrowed. "And you barely seem half that to me."

"It's because you're so old," she told him with mock seriousness. "Entering the golden years, where your bones creak and your eyesight is slowly dimming . . ."

"Damn you," he growled harshly. "Shut up!" His tone was venomous, so controlled that it seemed to shudder with sudden rage.

It was unexpected, and it silenced Keena immediately. She'd always teased Nicholas, from the beginning, and often about his age. He'd always laughed. But tonight she'd caught him on the raw for the first time, and he wasn't laughing. His face had snapped closed like something untamed. His eyes were the only things in his broad, hard face that seemed alive, and they were blazing with menace. She'd only seen Nicholas this angry once, when one of her coworkers had gotten miffed when she refused his advances. Nicholas had intended to surprise her in the office that day and had come in on them unexpectedly. Keena was sure that she could have subdued the young man without any help. But Nicholas, summing up the situation with a glance, had not stopped to ask for an invitation to rescue her. She'd learned later that he'd broken the young man's jaw. And ever since she'd carefully avoided antagonizing him.

Until now. And it hadn't been deliberate. "Nicholas, I was only teasing," she said softly.

That didn't calm him a bit. He picked up his wineglass with a grip that threatened to snap the slender stem and drained it in one huge gulp.

"Nicholas, please," she whispered, shivering

a little in the face of his white-hot anger. "Don't be angry with me."

He set the wineglass down with slow, deliberate movements before he pinned her with his eyes. "I'm forty, not eighty, and all the parts still work. If you don't believe that, ask Maria," he added icily.

She chewed on her lower lip. She hadn't meant to pull the lion's tail, but he was reacting in a way she'd never expected. Amazingly, she felt tears prick at her eyes and that was new too. She hadn't cried for years. But she felt tears damming up in her eyes now.

She put her napkin down very gently, avoiding Nicholas's blazing eyes. "Uh, if you don't mind, I've an early start tomorrow," she managed in a shadow of her normal tone.

"Would you like dessert?" he asked with glacial courtesy.

She stared at him with a brave but trembling arch in her chin. "Only if I get to pour it over your head," she managed with dripping sweetness.

For an instant, amusement vied with anger in his face, but it was quickly subdued. "Let's go then," he said.

She preceded him out of the restaurant after he'd paid the check, walking quickly, her slender legs rippling the sensuous velvet of her dress, her head held as regally as a princess's.

"Careful you don't sprain your neck," he chided.

"Your temper's more in danger of a sprain than my neck is," she countered coolly. "If you'd rather brood for a while, I can get a cab back to my apartment," she added. "I've had a pretty rotten day so far, and tonight isn't making up for it."

"Stop it," he growled, nodding to Jimson as they reached the car. He opened the door for Keena as Jimson got in under the wheel and cranked the engine.

"I didn't start it," she returned, avoiding his hand as she got into the seat that he was holding the door open to. She moved as far away from him as possible when he got in beside her and closed the door.

"Don't pout, for God's sake," he shot at her with a hard glare.

She returned the glare with interest. It was the first major argument they'd had, and it was beginning to set records for antagonism.

"I'll pout if I damn please!" she flared up, hunched in her corner. "Why don't you go find Maria if you want a sparring partner? I didn't try to lure you into my bed and then refuse to let you go when you were tired of me."

"You wouldn't know what to do with me if you got me into your bed," he returned with malice.

She started to make a smart remark back, but she was suddenly too tired to make the effort. It had been a perfectly horrible day, and it was just getting worse. Now her only friend was furious with her, and she wanted to wail.

They rode in a tense silence until Jimson pulled up at the curb in front of her apartment house and sat looking straight ahead while Keena reached for the doorknob.

But a big, warm hand got there first, holding hers where it rested on the handle.

"Not like this," he said heavily, his tone strained. "I can't leave for Europe tomorrow with a sword between us."

"Why not?" she countered, not looking at him. "I've seen you walk away from worse—and laugh."

"Not you," he said quietly. *"Never* you."

The tone of his voice more than the words calmed her. She turned slowly and looked up at him. He was closer than she'd realized, his dark eyes only inches away, the warmth and fragrance of his big body permeating her, drowning her in sensation.

"I don't think you're old," she whispered unsteadily, affected by him as she'd never been before. "I've never paid any attention to the age difference; it never mattered."

His dark eyes searched hers with a scrutiny that made her nervous. "Tease me about my size, or my money, or my temper. But leave birthdays out of it from now on."

She swallowed. "All right, Nicholas."

He removed his hand from hers as if it burned him. "I'll see you when I get back. It may take two weeks to close this deal, so don't expect me before the middle of February."

Two weeks without him. The bleak winter was going to move even slower until he returned, and she was just realizing how empty her life was going to be without those unexpected visits and phone calls. He'd been away from the city for long periods before and it hadn't bothered her. But suddenly it did, and she looked up at him with a curious frown above her pale green eyes.

"You look strange," he remarked.

"We haven't argued in a long time. In fact, I don't really think we ever did," she said gently, her eyes troubled.

"Perhaps we're more aware of each other now," he said, his voice unusually quiet as he looked down into her eyes.

"Aware?" she whispered.

His breath came hard and quick as he looked down at her soft mouth with an intensity that made her heart race. It was as if he were kissing it, and her lips parted involuntarily, her eyes half-closed at the intensity of the gaze.

"I can almost feel your mouth under mine, do you know that?" he murmured in a voice like deep velvet. "Your lips trembling, your breasts swelling against me . . ."

"Nicholas!" she burst out, half-gasping, half-angry, at the intimacy of it.

"If Jimson wasn't sitting up front trying not to see us, I'd give you a damned sight more than words to remember me by," he growled harshly. "I'd wrestle you down on the seat and teach you things about your body you've never dreamed it could feel. And you want it," he added with a level gaze that made her knees melt. "Don't you?"

Her body was trembling madly. She gaped at him, hating her own reactions, hating him for sensing them.

"You're my friend," she choked.

"I'm going to be your lover," he replied curtly. "Think about that while I'm gone."

She got out of the car quickly, almost tripping in her haste while Nicholas sat there and watched her with unholy amusement, his eyes glittering with triumph. He knew how he affected her. He had too much experience, damn him, not to know.

"Maybe I won't be here when you get back," she cried with a pitiful attempt at self-preservation, at pride.

"You'll be here," he said, and closed the door.

"You'll be lucky," she muttered as the elegant taillights of the Rolls disappeared into the night. She didn't realize how prophetic the words were. The next morning, her father's doctor called to tell her that her only surviving relative had been found dead in his bed. Her father was gone.

The funeral had been harrowing, and Keena was grateful when it was over at last, when her father's few well-meaning friends had gone and the house was finally peaceful.

She thumbed through the documents on his desk with a faint smile. It had been so like him to leave everything neat, in order. It was almost as if he'd expected the massive coronary that had taken his life.

The will was just as straightforward as Alan Whitman had always been. It left the house to Keena, along with pitifully few possessions. It saddened her that the entire estate barely amounted to the profits her business realized in one day.

She got up from the desk and stood at the window. Her father had never allowed her to give him any money to provide him with even a new car. He and his daughter had been close, but like her he valued his independence. He wanted nothing that he hadn't earned himself, although he was pleased with her success and frequently told her so.

She looked through the window at the narrow road that ran by the front of the house to the small town beyond. How many of her old classmates would know her now? she wondered. In adolescence she'd been a gangly, painfully shy girl with clothes that always seemed to hang on her, and an eternal slump. Most of the other students had laughed at her, boys and girls alike, and had made fun of the way she dressed, the walk that they said had the grace of a pelican running. She was as out of place in the small town as a sparrow would have been in a den of hawks. Alan Whitman had moved here from Miami, settling in this pleasant section of south Georgia with a mind toward starting his own business. But illness had slowed him down, diminished his resources, and he'd had a daughter to support. So he'd taken a job at the local textile mill, just until he could get on his financial feet again. But he'd been trapped by house payments and car payments and doctor bills into keeping the hated job, and he'd found all too soon that there was no way out. He was stuck.

His spirit was all but broken by the long hours, and there was no laughter in the big house he'd spent his life savings on. He had dozens of get-rich-quick schemes that fell through quickly. He spent his life looking for the rainbow, but all he found was the pants line of the manufacturing company.

Keena sighed bitterly at the irony of life. Her father had got poor making clothes, while she'd got rich. Even now she looked the part of the wealthy career woman in her chic designer jeans and wide-sleeved silk blouse. The emeralds on her ears and her wrist were real, not the paste ones she'd loved to wear as a poor teenager.

How long ago it all seemed now, those brief, secret meetings with him in the woods, the first few kisses that led a naive Keena to an apartment owned by one of James's friends. Tall, dark-headed, with vivid blue eyes under thick black lashes, James Harris had been the darling of the social set, a young attorney with promise. Keena had known that it was disastrous to care about him, but her heart had ignored her mind and gone end over end every time it saw him. She couldn't begin to look at another boy, or even Larry Harris, who worshipped her.

If only she'd realized that he had never had any intention of marrying her. She'd been too blinded by her own feelings to realize that James was keeping his relationship with her a secret from everyone. He'd never even stopped by the house to see her, or pick her up there for one of their few dates, and he was careful to stay away from public places. They spent long hours in his car at the local lovers' lane, necking, until one night when the kisses grew suddenly longer and slower and deeper, and he suggested that they go to his friend's apartment to have a snack before he took her home. They both knew why they were going, and it had nothing to do with food. Keena, young and naive and with her first passion for a man in full bloom, went trustingly.

She was expecting all the fiery passion and tenderness of every romantic novel she had read. But James, for a supposedly practiced lover, was carelessly intent on his own satisfaction. He hadn't even bothered with taking time to study the softly curving young body he'd taken so quickly and roughly.

"Get your clothes on fast," he'd said the minute he was through, leaving Keena confused, frustrated, and ashamed of her easy capitulation. He didn't even look at her as he dressed. "Hurry!" he'd called over his shoulder. "Jack could come in any minute. He told me I could only have the apartment for an hour."

She'd dressed hurriedly, tears streaming from her eyes, her body feeling bruised, violated. She'd expected a loving word or two, but there had been none of that.

She'd followed him to the door, and he'd taken her back to the end of her driveway, careful to stop the car in the privacy of the alley so that no one would recognize it.

"Sorry I had to be so quick," he'd said with a half smile. "Next time it will be better. I'll find another place."

There wasn't going to be a next time, and she'd told him so, her voice shaking with disappointment.

"Well, what did you expect, rose petals and fireworks?" he'd burst out. "I thought you cared about me."

"I did," she'd wept.

"I don't want any part of your fears, Keena. There are too many willing girls." And he'd driven away.

Keena had sweated out the next few weeks, and she hadn't relaxed until she knew she wasn't pregnant. But her love for James hadn't eased. She watched for him; she listened for the phone. But he didn't even try to get in touch with her. In desperation she accepted his brother Larry's invitation to a party at the Harris home, hoping for just a sight of James, a sign that he wasn't really through with her. It had just been an argument, after all. He'd talked about marriage, about an engagement. Perhaps he was giving her time to think. Of course, that was why he hadn't called. And all that gossip about James and Cherrie was just that—gossip. So what that Cherrie was the daughter of a prominent local attorney, and a voluptuous blonde? It was Keena that James really cared for.

She accepted Larry's invitation, wondering if he knew how she felt about his brother, if that might account for that odd, vague pity she often read in his eyes. In later years she'd wondered, because Larry had seemed to wait deliberately until she was in earshot to talk to James the night of the party.

She'd wore a dress of white crepe which she'd made from material bought with money she earned working in the local grocery store at the checkout counter. Even then, she'd had a flair for fashion, creating her own design. The dress had caused a mild sensation, even on a mill worker's daughter. But James had only spared her a sharp glance when she'd walked in on Larry's arm. He hadn't asked her to dance or greeted her. Neither had his father or mother, in fact, unless those cold smiles and curt nods could be classified as such.

She'd been only a few feet away when she heard Larry ask James, "Doesn't Keena look like a dream tonight?"

"I hadn't noticed," came the terse reply. "Why in hell did you have to invite her here tonight? Mother may play Lady Bountiful to the workers, but she won't care much for her son dating one," James reminded him with a short, cold laugh. "Keena's father is, after all, just one of our spreaders. He isn't even an executive."

"He's nice," Larry had defended.

"My God, maybe he is, but he's as dull as a winter day, just like his skinny daughter. She's plain and stupid, and she's practically flat-chested to boot. Believe me, it was like making love to a man . . ."

She'd felt Larry's shock, even at a distance. "Making love?" he breathed.

Keena hadn't stayed to hear any more. With her eyes full of tears and her makeup running down her white face, she'd left the house and walked every step of the way home in the dark without thinking about danger. And those cold, hurting words had stayed with her ever since. They'd been indirectly responsible for her success, because her hatred for James Harris and her thirst for revenge had carried her through the lean, hard times that had led up to her enrollment in the fashion design school. All she'd wanted in life from that terrible night forward was to become something more than a mill worker's daughter—an outsider. And she had.

There was a discreet tap on the door before Mandy came in like a small, dark-haired whirlwind, her dark eyes sparkling.

"Brought you some coffee," she said, placing a tray on the coffee table. A plate of doughnuts rested temptingly beside it. "Come on, you've got to eat something."

Keena grimaced at her housekeeper. "I don't want food," she said. "Just coffee. You be a love and eat the doughnuts."

"You'll blow away," the older woman warned. "Why bother to bring me down here with you if you aren't going to let me cook?"

"It gets lonely here," she replied. She gazed around her at the towering near-ruin of a house. It must have been a showplace years before her father bought it, but lack of care and deterioration had taken their toll on it.

Without some substantial repairs, it was going to fall in.

"Did you reach the construction people?" Keena asked as she stirred cream into a cup of steaming coffee.

"Yes," Mandy replied, looking disapproving. "Look, it's none of my business, but why are you going to funnel good money into this white mausoleum?"

Keena ran a lazy hand over the faded, worn brocade of the antique sofa. "I'll need to have the furniture redone as well. See if you can find an upholsterer while you're at it."

"How long are we going to be here?" Mandy asked curiously.

"A few weeks." She laughed at Mandy's obvious shock. "I need a break. I can run the company from here; Ann can call me if she needs help. And meanwhile, I'll play with mending this pitiful house."

"I wish I knew what you were up to," Mandy sighed.

"It's a kind of game," Keena explained with a smile.

"And is Nicholas going to play too?"

Keena glared at her. She didn't want to think about Nicholas right now. "He's a friend, nothing more. Just because we go out once in a while . . ."

"Twice a week, every week, and he protects you like a mother hen," Mandy corrected.

Keena shifted uneasily. "Nick's like a brother. He feels responsible for me."

"Some brother," Mandy scoffed. "You should have noticed the way he was watching you at that Christmas party we gave. He started scowling every time another man came near you. He'll be along, Miss Independence, or I miss my guess. No way is Nicholas going to let you spend several weeks down here without doing something about it."

"What do you expect him to do, come and drag me back home?" Keena asked curtly.

"I wouldn't put it past him," came the equally brusque reply.

"You," Keena told her with a mock scowl, "are a professional busybody."

Mandy grinned. "Thanks. About time you paid me a compliment or two for these gray hairs you've given me."

Keena laughed, studying the little salt-and-pepper head. "Not so gray," she returned.

"You going to see that Harris man?" Mandy asked suddenly with narrowed eyes.

Keena met that gaze levelly. "Maybe."

"Good thing, too. Get him out of your system once and for all." She wiped her hands on her apron. "Memories are dangerous, you know. They're always better than reality."

"That's why I came back to face them," Keena admitted.

She stretched hugely and got up from the sofa. "We've been getting some interested glances since I had the corral and stable fences repaired and bought that mare." She smiled. "I think I'll go for a ride."

"Didn't you tell me once that this property joins the Harrises'?" Mandy asked.

"In back," Keena agreed. "I used to rent a horse to ride. I saved all my money just to catch a glimpse of James Harris in the woods. Maybe I'll get lucky today," she added with a smile and a wink.

It was chilly in the woods, and Keena was glad of her jodhpurs and boots, the thick cashmere sweater she put on over her silk blouse, the warm fur-lined gloves on her hands, and the thick tweed hacking jacket. She'd never been able to afford a decent kit in her youth, so it was something of a thrill to be able to wear it now. It almost made up for those rides she'd gone on with Jenny Harris, James's sister, in worn jeans and a denim jacket that Jenny was too sweet to make fun of.

She paused by a small stream, her eyes

closed, taking in the cold, sweet peace of the woods, the sound of water running between the banks, the sudden snapping of twigs nearby.

Her eyes flew open as another horse and rider came into view. A big black horse with a slender man astride him, a dark-haired man with blue eyes and an unsmiling face. He was wearing a tweed jacket, too, over a turtleneck sweater. The hands on the reins were long-fingered, and a cigarette dangled in one of them.

"You're trespassing," the man said. "This is private property."

She lifted an eyebrow at him, ignoring the wild beat of her heart as she felt the ten years between her last sight of him fall away.

"The property line is two paces behind you," she replied coolly. "And if you care to look, there's a metal survey stake—quite a new one. I had the property lines resurveyed two days ago."

His eyes narrowed as he lowered them to her slender body, past her high, firm breasts to her small waist and flaring hips, clearly outlined by her tailored riding gear.

"Keena?" he asked, as if the thought was incredulous. His eyes came back up to her lovely, high-cheekboned face framed by black hair that feathered around it, her pale green eyes like clear pools under her thick lashes.

She allowed herself a smile. "That's my name."

"My God, you've changed," he murmured. His eyes went to her wrist, and he smiled faintly. "Except for that habit of wearing gaudy costume jewelry. I'm glad something about you hasn't changed."

She wanted to hit him with the riding crop, but that would have been more in character in her adolescence than it was now. She'd learned control, if nothing else.

"Old habits die hard," she replied with a bitter smile.

"How true," he murmured. "I was sorry to hear about your father. He was a good worker. There's a small insurance policy, of course. You might check with the personnel office about that. You got the flowers we sent? A potted plant, I think . . ."

"They were very nice, thanks," she replied.

"Are you still living in Atlanta?" he asked politely.

"New York," she corrected.

He made a distasteful face. "Nasty place. Pollution and all that. I prefer Ashton."

She stared at him, letting the memory merge with the reality. He'd changed. Not just in age, but in every other way. He looked older, less imposing, less authoritative.

"How's Jenny?" she asked quietly.

"Doing very well, thanks. She lives with her husband and son in Greenville. Larry's married," he added pointedly. "He lives in Charleston."

"I heard that you and Cherrie married," she said.

His face drew up. "She and I were divorced two years back," he said coldly.

She shrugged. "It happens."

He was staring at her again, his eyes thoughtful. "I can't get over the change. You're different."

"I'm older," she replied.

"Married?" he asked, openly curious.

She shook her head. "I have a career."

"In textiles?" he asked with a faint smile.

She paused. "In a matter of speaking, yes."

He laughed shortly. "Sewing, I suppose."

"That too." She patted the mare's mane. "I've got to get back. Nice seeing you," she said with a parting smile.

"I'll drop by before you leave for home," he said unexpectedly.

She gave him her best smile. "That would be nice," she managed huskily. "But you needn't rush. I'll be here for several more weeks."

44

His eyebrows shot up. "Can you spare that long from your job?"

"I have a wonderful, understanding boss," she returned. "See you."

And think about that, she laughed to herself as she let the mare have her head on the way back to the stable.

What Ashton needed, she decided, was a party. A big, lavish, New York, society-type party, so that she could show her dear old friends how much the gangly textile worker's daughter had changed. Just thinking about it brightened her dark mood. Before she got back to the house, she was already planning her strategy, from redecorating and renovation, to the caterers. This was going to be an absolute delight.

It was like having a houseful of relatives come to stay when the carpenters and decorators descended on them. Keena couldn't move without bumping into a ladder or a pile of lumber.

"They're multiplying," Mandy moaned one morning, watching two carpenters hard at work trying to replace a portion of the kitchen ceiling. "And how can I cook?"

"Make two plates full of sandwiches," Keena laughed. "Maybe if we feed them enough, they'll work faster. And don't spare the coffee."

"You're the boss," Mandy sighed, shaking her head as she moved toward the cupboard.

"Hey, lady, somebody's at the door!" one of the electricians called, pausing with a length of cord in one hand.

She squeezed past a painter on a ladder, her jeans and pale blue T-shirt making her look younger than her years, clinging outrageously to her long, graceful legs and the soft, full curves of her body. Her hair was curling softly around her face, and some of the strain of big business had fallen away despite the grief this trip had started with. She felt younger, more relaxed, and more feminine.

"Hey, guys, there's a Rolls-Royce out there!" one of the carpenters whispered to his friends, stunned.

Keena paused with her hand on the doorknob. It couldn't be James Harris, even though that was whom she'd expected after their confrontation two days ago. The Harrises had money, but not enough to run a Rolls. She knew only one man with that kind of careless wealth, and she hadn't dreamed—despite Mandy's prediction—that he'd come here.

She twisted the crystal doorknob and pulled

the wide door open. The man standing there towered over her, as broad as a wrestler, all hard muscle and determination, with a craggy face and dark eyes that were devouring every inch of her.

"So here you are," he growled, his voice reminiscent of the last time she'd seen him, and remembering it made her flush slightly. "I've had a hell of a time finding you. Mrs. Barnes said you called the apartment to see if I'd come home, but all you told her was that you were going home to Georgia."

"And you couldn't remember where that was?" she asked with a sweet smile.

"It's a damned big state," he replied curtly, staring past her at the gaping workmen who were openly curious about the newcomer in the gray suit. "I had to hunt through your old personnel file to find out your hometown. I couldn't remember it."

"You didn't think to call my office?" she asked.

"I got back only yesterday," he said under his breath. "Sunday, madam, and your people don't work on Sunday."

She drew in a steadying breath. Seeing him again was causing her heart to do acrobatics. "My father died," she said quietly.

"I'm sorry," he said curtly. "Was it quick?"

She nodded. "Very." She looked up at him with sad eyes, and wished she could have run to him when they'd called to tell her. His arms would have felt so good, and she could have cried in them. "Did you think I was in hiding?" she added with a mirthless laugh.

"Hide, here?" He glared at the workmen. "You'd have hell trying with this crowd. It looks like a damned construction site in here."

"Would you like to come in?" she asked.

"My insurance company wouldn't like it," he said bluntly, with a wary eye on the two carpenters up on ladders just inside the open door.

"Well, we could sit in the porch swing," she suggested, gesturing toward it.

His eyes followed hers. Two boards were missing in strategic places. His dark eyes danced and just for an instant she caught a glimpse of something different in them.

"Not unless you want to sit on my lap and give your audience something to stare at," he replied. "Besides that, it's blasting cold out here, and you aren't dressed for it." He caught her arm. "We'll sit in the car and talk for a minute."

"Lecherous thing," she murmured, following him to the car quickly to get out of the biting cold. "You'll probably lock me in and try to seduce me."

"There's an idea," he agreed, putting her in the passenger side of the Rolls. "Slide over."

She made room for him, feeling swallowed as he slid one huge arm around her and gave her the benefit of his warmth against the faint chill of the car.

"Some idea," she murmured. "You've never even made a real pass at me."

He leaned down, his face suddenly closer than it had ever been before, so close that she could see the tiny lines at the corners of his eyes, the thickness of his eyelashes, the faint shadow around his firm, chiseled mouth. An expensive fragrance, a familiar fragrance, clung to his big warm body.

"You never wanted it before," he reminded her. His eyes went to her mouth, pale without lipstick, and her heart rocked at the sensuous look in his glittering eyes. "Not until the night I left for Paris. But this is as good a time as any to satisfy your curiosity, little Miss Purity. Let me show you how I kiss."

He leaned closer, brushing his parted lips against hers before she had time to protest. The tenderness of the action paralyzed her, and in a trance, she watched his mouth touch and lift and brush against hers in a silence that was suddenly sparkling and alive with new sensations, new awareness.

His strong white teeth nipped softly at her lips, tugging them deftly apart as his tongue tasted, slowly, the inner curve of her upper lip.

She gasped at the contact, her eyes looking straight into his, seeing shadows that had never been there before.

"You taste of coffee," he said in a deep, sensuous tone.

"I . . . had it . . . for breakfast." Was that her voice, that high-pitched, husky stammer? She felt as rigid as a board, tense, waiting for something with a hunger that was as shocking as the look on Nicholas's face.

"I think I'll have you for breakfast," he murmured, and she watched his mouth open slightly as it fitted itself expertly to her soft, tremulous lips. "Open your mouth," he whispered against the silken softness. "Don't make me force you."

"Nicholas?" His name came out as a gasp when she felt his big warm hands cupping her face, barely aware of his body half-covering hers, crushing her back against the soft leather in a warm, breathless embrace.

He didn't answer her. His mouth was hard and warm and faintly cruel as it moved with slow deliberation deeper and deeper into hers. Her heart felt as if it were on a merry-go-round. She was spinning, flying.

"Oh," she whispered, shaken, into the hard mouth laying claim to her lips.

His tongue went into her mouth, teasing, withdrawing, causing sensations she'd only dreamed about before. Something devastating was happening to her.

One of his big warm hands left her cheek and eased down to the soft cotton fabric over her breast. He took the weight of it into his cupped palm, savoring its softness, testing its firmness, and she gasped at the newness of his touch, drawing back to look into his dark eyes.

"You don't wear a bra, do you?" he asked in a slow, tender voice. "You don't need one either. Your breasts are so soft, Keena, firm and soft and warm under my hands."

"Nick . . ." she gasped, drowning in the sure touch of his fingers, probing, caressing.

She caught his hand and stilled it, half-frightened.

"Please, don't," she whispered. "Nick . . ."

"I like the way you say my name," he murmured deeply. "Say it again."

She felt like a fish out of water, floundering. She couldn't get her breath at all, and her mouth throbbed with both his possession of it and her own hunger to have him do it again. She lowered her eyes to his white shirt.

"Shy of me?" he asked softly. "After all these years?"

She looked up at him warily. "We've never made love before," she whispered unsteadily, keenly aware of his fingers still resting lightly on her breast.

"I wouldn't call this making love," he corrected quietly, studying her wild eyes. "Why don't you want me to touch you?"

She blushed furiously, hating her foolishness, her lack of sophistication, hating his mocking laughter.

"You liked it, didn't you?" he asked, removing his hand to ruffle her dark hair.

"I've got to go back inside," she ground out.

"Not yet. When was the funeral?"

"A week ago."

He scowled. "And you're still here?" His eyes narrowed. "Why?"

Her lips compressed stubbornly. She wasn't going to be talked out of this, not now. She told him why she was staying, in no uncertain terms, tacking on, "And the first guest I'm inviting to the party is James Harris."

His dark eyes seemed to burst with flame as he stared down at her.

He knew that Keena had loved James Harris and that he had hurt her badly because Keena had cried her heart out on his shoulder one night after too many whiskey sours on an empty stomach—one of those rare occasions when she drank hard liquor. But he'd never learned exactly what Harris had done to her to cause her so much pain. All he knew was that he'd never let James Harris hurt her again.

"You're crazy as hell if you think I'm going to let that creep get his hands on you," he said in a cutting voice.

"And just what do you think you're going to do about it, Nicholas?" she demanded with more courage than she felt. The long, searching kiss and the touch of his big hands had knocked half the fight out of her.

He moved away from her, got out of the car, and stood back to let her get out of the car. "I fight with no holds barred," he reminded her with a strange, cool smile. "And I've put in a lot of years on you. I'm not about to stand by and watch you put your pretty neck into a noose."

"It's my neck," she murmured.

He tilted her chin up and bent down to her, brushing his mouth slowly, softly against hers with something like possession in his dark eyes. He watched her helpless reaction with a smile. "I told you before I left for Paris that one day I was going to be your lover. That day's closer than you think, sweetheart, and you're hungrier for me than I'd imagined. Ripe, ready to be picked."

"I'm not an apple," she ground out.

"No, you're a peach," he corrected with a last, soft kiss. "A sweet, juicy little peach that I could eat. But first I'm going to have to knock you out of the tree."

She glared at him as he went around the elegant hood of the Rolls and got in under the steering wheel. "You'd better get a big stick, Nicholas Coleman!" she cried.

He only laughed. "No, honey, you had. I'll be back."

And before she could fire a retort, he drove off in a cloud of dust, leaving her standing there in the cold.

Three

Mandy glanced up from the rolls she was making in the kitchen as Keena walked through.

"Flames," she murmured, muffling a grin.

"What?" Keena asked absently, unaware of the picture she made with her hair mussed from Nick's big fingers, her eyes wild, her lips swollen and red.

"Coming from you," Mandy commented dryly. She started laying the rolls into a pan. "Seen Nick, have you?"

"Seen him?" she burst out. "You should have heard . . ." She flushed. "On second thought, you shouldn't have heard him. But he's absolutely unreasonable!"

"How?"

"He doesn't want me to stay here, for one thing," she muttered darkly, her lovely eyes narrowing. She folded her arms across her throbbing chest and leaned back against the counter. "As if he had any right, any right at all, to order me around. The nerve, talking about knocking me out of trees and getting sticks . . ."

"You feel all right?" Mandy asked pleasantly.

"No. Yes. I don't know."

"That's what I've always liked most about you—your definite answers," Mandy grinned.

Keena, not even half-hearing her housekeeper, turned in a daze and walked under the ladder where two painters were busy on the walls and ceiling of the dining room. She was confused as she'd never been, as shy as a girl when she thought about seeing Nicholas again after that ardent kiss. He'd touched her. . . .

She sighed, walking aimlessly up the stairs with dreams in her eyes. In all those years, not a single pass, not a touch out of the way, but overnight, her whole relationship with Nick was different, exciting. He'd been her friend, but now what was he? She was going to have to rethink her entire relationship with him after today.

Funny, she hadn't really taken him seriously the night he left for Paris, when he'd said that he was going to be her lover. Reflecting on it, she'd decided that he'd been teasing. But today was no joke. The tenderness of the mouth he'd kissed so thoroughly was very real, and her chest tingled from the long, hard contact with his big body, from the touch of his experienced hands.

Part of her, a small, vague part, was afraid of Nicholas. He wasn't the kind of man to do anything half-heartedly. He wouldn't stop at acquiring her for his bed. He'd want nothing less than possession. Keena liked her independence; she wasn't sure she was ready to give it up. In that, she must have been like her mother, who died giving her birth. Alan Whitman had always spoken fondly of his late wife's bullheaded independence. Keena was like that herself. She'd been on her own for so long, an achiever without props. Oh, there had been men; charming, attractive companions that she had always managed to keep at a safe distance—no ties, no commitments. She'd let them know that it would be on her terms, or not at all. No, she wasn't at all sure she could

57

manage a full-time man in her life, especially a man like Nick, in an intimate relationship. She had no doubts at all after today that he'd be everything her body would ever want. But what about the rest of her? Would he try to take her over the way he took over businesses? And if she let herself be drawn into his life, would she ever be able to break away before it was too late? She was afraid to let him close enough to find out. Perhaps it was just as well that he'd gone back to New York. But it wasn't like Nicholas to give up without a struggle. She had a feeling she hadn't heard the last of it either.

"How old were you when you left here?" Mandy asked several days later when Keena was driving her through town in the rented car, pointing out the small high school, the public library, and the modest shopping center near the house.

"Eighteen," Keena said, veiling the memories that the admission dredged up. They weren't pleasant ones, for the most part.

"You must have missed it," Mandy smiled, watching two young boys ride their bicycles along the sidewalk, bundled up from head to toe against the February chill. "It's a lovely little town."

"Lovely," came the absent reply.

The older woman glanced at her. "You're quiet lately. Brooding because Nick hasn't come back?" she probed dryly.

Keena's face toasted. "Of course not!"

"Don't run over the curb, love. You'll crease the tires," Mandy pointed out.

Keena steered the car back onto the road, hating that momentary, telling lapse. "Why should I care that he comes storming down here, threatens me, and then vanishes into the woodwork? It's no worry of mine!"

"Oh, that's obvious."

"Besides, it's my life," Keena added firmly, shifting uneasily behind the wheel. "I can do what pleases me."

"Sure you can."

"If I want to decorate the house and give a party, it's my own business."

"That's right, dear."

"And, anyway, if he cares so much, why hasn't he called?" Keena's green eyes flashed. "He could have spared time for a phone call."

"He's a busy man."

"I'm busy too," Keena pouted. She sighed, the action gently rustling the blue striped scarf at her neck that complemented her navy pant-suit and white silk blouse. "He's just sour because I'm not at his beck and call down here."

"He's jealous of James Harris, you mean," Mandy remarked with a secret smile.

"There's nothing to be jealous of. James hasn't called, he hasn't come by the house . . ." That rankled too. She'd been a very young eighteen when she'd overheard that bitter speech of James's, when she'd realized just how fully she'd been taken in by his teasing and flirting. She'd been too naive to realize the cruel game he was playing until it was too late. Part of her hadn't grown past that day. And that part, the hurting part, wanted to bring the tall, blue-eyed lawyer to his knees. It was something inside her that she didn't fully understand, but it was too strong to ignore. Nicholas might tolerate the thirst for revenge, but he wouldn't tolerate its presence around him. He didn't need it. Nick was above that sort of pettiness. But Keena didn't find it petty, and she needed to see James Harris humbled, as she had once been. Now, successful, full of confidence she'd never had as a teenager, she was desirable. And she wanted James to find her so, to satisfy a craving that had never completely died. She had to prove to herself that she could have him if she really wanted him. And no one, not even Nick, was going to stop her.

* * *

She'd just worked up her nerve to call James and invite him over for a meal when she drove up in front of her house to find him waiting for her. Her heart jumped wildly at the sight of him in an expensive tweed coat with a sweater-vest and dark trousers. He looked sophisticated, handsome, and not a day older than he had nine years ago.

"Speak of the devil," Mandy murmured, rushing out of the car and up the steps before Keena had time to reply.

"So there you are." James grinned, hopping down the steps as he used to, athletic and trim. "I thought you might invite me in for coffee if I showed up at your door. Quite a crowd of workmen you've got there," he added, nodding toward the carpenters at work on the outside of the house.

"We're adopting them; they're orphans," she told him with a straight face.

He threw back his head and laughed. It didn't sound genuine somehow, but Keena laughed with him. "Uh, Jones said you'd borrowed quite a lot of money to accomplish this," he added shrewdly.

She only smiled. She could have paid cash for the renovation, but it had done her good to borrow the money from Abraham Jones at James's bank, leaving that priceless emerald bracelet as collateral. She'd expected it to get back to James. Now he was curious, and that was just what she'd wanted.

"That bracelet," he murmured, looking at her with his head cocked to one side in that old, familiar pose. "It was real, wasn't it?"

"Quite," she agreed with a wry smile.

"A present?" he probed.

"No."

He frowned, really puzzled now. "I can't figure you out," he admitted finally.

She smiled up at him, turning on every trace of charm in her slender body. "Can't you really, James?" she asked softly.

Something kindled in his blue eyes, something new and pleasant. He moved toward her, removing his hands from his pockets to take her gently by the shoulders and study her lazily.

"You've changed so," he remarked gently. "You were pretty before. But now . . ."

"Now, James?" she prodded, breathless.

He opened his mouth to speak just as the soft purr of an approaching engine broke into the silence between them.

Keena turned her head in time to see Nicholas bring the white Rolls to a gentle stop and get out, carrying a big leather suitcase in one hand and an attaché case in the other. He was dressed in an expensive tweed suit that flattered his massive physique, emphasizing his broad chest, flat stomach, and powerful, muscular legs. He not only looked rich, he looked imposing. His eyes punctuated the threat in the graceful way he moved, the way he looked at James, the way a hunter might glance toward a kitten on his way to shoot bear.

"I hope you've got a room ready," Nicholas told Keena without breaking stride. "I'm in a hell of a tangle with my London office."

She stared after him, her mouth slightly open.

"Who's he?" James asked coolly.

Keena looked up at him helplessly. For one wild second she wondered if he might believe Nicholas was her insurance agent. But with a sigh, a shrug, and an apologetic smile, she dismissed the thought.

"Nicholas," she replied instead. "Uh, I've got to go, James, but do ring me later on."

"Oh . . . of course," he stammered. It was the first time Keena had ever seen him at a loss for words, as if he couldn't believe any woman would willingly part with his company.

She turned and walked quickly up the steps with blood in her eyes. Now what was Nicholas up to? And where did he plan to stay?

She caught up with him at the foot of the staircase, oblivious to the stares of the two fascinated painters on ladders in the hall.

"Where do you think you're going?" she demanded.

"To my room," he said impatiently.

"You don't have one," she pointed out.

"Yet," he admitted, taking another step.

"This is my house," she told him, her voice rising shrilly. "You can't just move in like this, without even asking!"

"Think you can stop me?" he asked politely, gazing at her with that level, devastating stare that made her want to back away slowly.

"I'm not alone and defenseless," she reminded him, turning to the nearest painter, a rugged-looking individual about Nicholas's age.

"That's right, lady," the painter agreed, pausing with his brush raised to give Nicholas his best threatening look.

Nicholas lifted his hard, broad face and stared up at the man unblinkingly. "I hope your insurance is current," he remarked politely.

The painter turned back to his work and began painting with a vengeance. "Like I said, lady, I'd give the poor tired man a room," he murmured sheepishly.

Keena glared at him before she transferred her irritated stare to the other painter, who pulled his cap low over his eyes and began to whistle softly.

Nicholas grinned at her before he turned and started up the staircase again.

She followed along behind him, her temper exploding like silent fireworks inside her taut body, watching helplessly while he peeked into the first room he came to, then the second, before he finally settled on the third. It was, as he had guessed, unoccupied, with bed linen neatly piled at the foot of the large, four-poster bed.

"This will do," he murmured, glaring around him at the antique furniture. He set the suitcase down and went to the window. "Nice view. Does it have a bathroom?"

"In between this bedroom and the other one," Keena said. "But that needn't concern you; you aren't staying."

He turned around and let his eyes roam over her taut figure. "God, you're pretty when you want to bite. Come over here and put up your fists, you little firecracker," he taunted in a deep, velvety voice.

"What are you doing here?" she challenged, feeling the ground slowly being cut from under her feet.

He shrugged. "What does it look like? I'm moving in."

"For how long?" she demanded fiercely.

"For as long as it takes to bring you to your senses," he replied calmly. His dark eyes searched her flushed face. "You can't go back, honey," he added quietly. "I won't let you."

Her color deepened. "I don't know what you mean."

"Yes, you do." He moved forward, one corner of his firm, chiseled mouth going up as he noticed her involuntary step backward. "Don't panic. I'm not going to throw you on the bed. Not now, anyway. I've got work to do. Is there a study?"

"Downstairs," she managed through her fury. "But it's full of painters."

"So is the rest of the house. Are they leaving, or are you adopting them?"

"They'll be gone tomorrow," she replied. "Nicholas, you can't stay here," she added, trying to reason with him. "It's a small town. People will go wild gossiping. They'll think you're my lover!"

"They might be right," he said, moving forward again. "Come here."

"Nicholas!" She backed right up to the closed door.

He trapped her there with his big arms on

either side of her head, his eyes dancing with devilish amusement, the shimmering depths secretive, mysterious. "Shy?" he murmured. "You were flirting with Harris for all you were worth. Why not try it with me?"

"Because I don't want to be fitted with a straitjacket, and how did you know it was James?" she asked nervously. The deliciously expensive scent of his cologne settled around her like a sensuous mist, and she tried not to be so aware of the size and strength of his body, the heat of it warming her in the faint chill of the room.

"I recognized the sickening adoration in your eyes, little fox," he murmured. His dark eyes pinned hers. "You may think you can pick up where you left off all those years ago, but you're going to find that it's not possible."

"It's my life, Nicholas," she reminded him.

"So it is," he agreed. "But I'm not going to let that anemic snob cut you up a second time."

She tried to get closer to the door, but the cold wood wouldn't give under her shoulder blades.

"I do appreciate the thought," she said. "But how are you going to spare the time?" She didn't like the look in his eyes. It was frankly predatory. "As you're so fond of telling me, you're a busy man."

His eyes glittered with amusement. "All work and no play . . ." he murmured, bending.

She watched his face come closer with a nervous sense of inevitability. *No wonder he'd gotten so far in business,* she thought dimly as his mouth brushed lightly against her forehead. He was unstoppable, like a runaway locomotive.

"You'll go through that door in a minute," he murmured lazily. "Why don't you move toward me instead?"

"You're making me nervous," she choked. Her lovely eyes had a faintly haunted look, her black hair was brushed with fiery lights in the glare of the window.

"Is that what it is?" he murmured. He moved, holding her eyes while he eased the full weight of his flat stomach and powerful thighs down against her as he guided her slender body down on the bed. She felt the warm, heavy crush with a sense of awe. She'd never been so close to him before, felt so overwhelmed by him. The kiss they'd shared in the Rolls, as ardent as it was, couldn't compare with the sensations this was causing. She'd never dreamed that she could drown in her awareness like this.

His powerful arms bent, and his chest

gently flattened her soft breasts. His watchful eyes never left hers, reading signs in them like an Indian after tracks.

She began to tremble under the contact. He had to feel it too.

"Nick . . ." she whispered brokenly.

"Fire and kindling," he whispered deeply, shifting his powerful body sensuously against hers. "We make flames when we touch like this."

A wave of intolerable sensation washed the length of her trapped body. Her hands, pressed helplessly against the warm front of his white shirt, began to move slowly, caressingly against the smooth, hard muscles.

"Nick," she moaned, her eyes half-closed, her body suddenly, involuntarily, answering his. She pressed closer, molding her body to fit the hard, sensuous contours of his. Her fingers curled under the top button of his shirt.

"Unbutton it, Keena," he murmured deeply, searching her eyes in the blazing, throbbing silence that stretched like a blanket around them. "Touch me."

Her eyes wandered in his while she took the pearly button out of the buttonhole and lightly touched the warm, hair-covered flesh underneath it. She felt the powerful muscles contract beneath her hands.

"You . . . feel like . . . warm stone," she whispered unsteadily, burying her fingers in the thick curling hair on his chest.

"I feel like a damned blazing inferno," he breathed, shifting his chest to enlarge the pattern of her caressing fingers. "My God, I've never wanted a woman's hands on me so much!"

She flinched at the sound of another voice merging with his, shattering like brittle glass as the spell was suddenly broken.

"Keena, I've got lunch!" Mandy was calling from the hallway.

A tiny sound burst from her tightly held lips, her eyes telling him how she felt about the intrusion.

His breath was coming as roughly as hers. "There'll be another time," he said tautly.

She managed a slow nod. He levered his body away from hers and moved to open the door.

"What are we having?" he asked Mandy, as composed as ever, one big hand unobtrusively closing the buttons Keena's searching fingers had loosed.

Mandy grinned at him, her hands buried in a dishcloth. "Your favorite," she said dryly, hiding a smile when she caught a glimpse of Keena's flushed face and wild eyes. "Beef Stroganoff, homemade rolls, a potato casserole, and fresh apple pie."

"Remind me to pry you away from Keena," he told her with a lazy wink.

"Can't split the set," came the murmured reply.

He chuckled. "I'm working on that."

Keena, a little more recovered now, moved around him and followed Mandy down the hall on rubbery legs without looking back. She couldn't meet Nicholas's mocking, confident gaze.

James called her later in the day to invite Keena to supper that night, his voice faintly caressing on the other end of the line.

"If your houseguest doesn't mind, of course," he added waspishly.

Keena's hand clenched on the receiver. "My . . . houseguest doesn't tell me what to do." She crossed her fingers involuntarily. "Nicholas is only a friend."

"If you say so. Does six o'clock suit you?" he added, a purr in his pleasant voice. "I thought we'd dine at the Magnolia Room."

She remembered the exclusive restaurant well. She'd ridden the bus past it on her way to Atlanta at the age of eighteen, when she'd left Ashton behind. She'd been crying, and through her tears she'd strained for a sight of James as the bus passed his favorite eating place.

"I'd like that," she murmured.

"See you at six, then."

She stared at the receiver when he hung up, wondering how she was going to explain it to Nicholas. She had a feeling it wasn't going to improve his mood.

Nicholas set up shop in the study and tied up the phone for the rest of the day. Keena could hear him growling through the closed door, and she was careful to keep out of his way. So were the painters, she noticed. Everyone walked wide around the study except Mandy, who darted in and out with coffee and pastries.

"Do you have to encourage him?" Keena asked once, only to be met by an innocent stare and raised eyebrows.

She went downstairs just five minutes before James was due to arrive, wearing a gown that she'd originally designed for a well-known actress—and then decided that something a little flashier would suit her client better. It was a green—more olive than emerald —deep, soft velvet with short puffed sleeves, an Empire waist, and a low neckline that relied on a hint of cleavage for its charm. The color mirrored that of her eyes, adding to the flush of her lips and cheeks, and the highlights in her freshly washed, curling short hair, an effect achieved with a blow dryer to make the ends turn toward her face. She eyed herself critically in the hall mirror. If this dress didn't set James on his ear, nothing would.

"Bewitching," Nicholas murmured from the doorway of the study.

She turned around, glaring at him. He was wearing his tweed slacks, but he'd discarded the jacket, and his silk tie hung loose across his chest, the top few buttons of his shirt undone. It was one of the few times she'd seen him when he didn't look impeccable and businesslike. His dark, shaggy mane was faintly rumpled and a forgotten cigarette smoldered in one big hand. Her fingers itched to touch him.

"Going somewhere?" he asked pleasantly.

She swallowed and straightened her elegant figure. "Out. With James," she added defiantly.

One dark eyebrow curled upward. "Oh?"

She stiffened at that mocking reply. Only Nicholas could mingle distaste, contempt, and reprisal in a single sound.

"He asked me out to dinner," she elaborated.

He studied the wisps of gray smoke that came between them. "I hope you don't plan on being out late," he remarked. "Waiting up for people makes me cranky."

"I'm twenty-seven," she reminded him. "Nobody waits up for me anymore, not even Mandy."

"Well, honey, I'll have to do something about that, won't I?" he asked with a mocking smile.

"Mandy will fix you something to eat," she replied.

"So she told me."

"There's James," she murmured, her ears picking up the sound of an approaching car.

He shouldered away from the door facing. "Have fun. While you can."

He went back into the study and closed the door.

The restaurant was the very best Ashton had to offer, spacious, elegant, with a hint of grandeur that would have taken Keena's breath away nine years ago. As it was, she murmured suitably as James seated her. But the sophisticated woman she'd become wasn't overly impressed, despite the company she was keeping.

James stared at her across the table when

the waiter had brought the menus, frowning thoughtfully, his blue eyes approving.

"What a change," he murmured softly, turning on the old charm she remembered so well.

A tiny thrill shot down her spine, but it was hardly the surge of pleasure she'd once imagined it would be to see that particular look in James's eyes. It was disappointing. She'd halfway expected the earth to move.

She shifted restlessly in her chair. Nicholas had upset her in more ways than one. What in the world was she going to do about him? By tomorrow his presence in her house would be the subject of early-morning gossip over half the coffee cups in town. Not that she minded gossip ordinarily, but she had plans, and Nicholas was going to upset them all if she didn't find some way to pry him out of her guest room.

"Did I say something wrong?" James asked, his tone one of concern.

She mentally pinched herself. "Of course not." She created just the right smile and reached out boldly to touch his long-fingered hand. "I'm having a marvelous time. Remember when this restaurant first opened? Mayor Henderson cut the ribbon, and the Lieutenant Governor was the first guest . . ."

"He was a friend of Max's," he recalled, referring to the restaurant's owner, Max Kells.

And not in my league back then, she thought dryly. "Tell me, how is Max?"

He shrugged. "Fine, I suppose. I've been too busy lately to socialize much." James stared at her thoughtfully across the table, breaking the gaze only long enough to give the waiter their order.

"You really have changed." He repeated himself. "Velvet gowns, sophisticated, worldly. Do you really work in textiles?"

"I started out there," she admitted. "But not on the floor. I'm a fashion designer now. My casual line sells to some of the most exclusive stores in the country—and abroad."

"So it isn't your . . . houseguest's money that's keeping you up?" he asked with careless bluntness.

It would be an obvious conclusion for someone who didn't know about her unusual relationship with Nicholas, but it brought back James's cruelty of years past with full force.

"No," she replied coolly. "Nicholas doesn't keep me."

"Nicholas?" he fished.

"Coleman," she provided. Her long, well-manicured fingers toyed with her crystal water glass. "Of Coleman Textiles," she added.

Both his eyebrows arched toward the ceiling. "Exalted company," he murmured.

"Isn't it?" she replied with a smile. Nicholas's vast holdings were hardly fair comparison for James's small company, which he ran along with his modest law practice. In fact, Nicholas could have bought it all out of what he'd term petty cash, and James knew it.

"Is he your lover?" James persisted with an interest that seemed casual, but that Keena knew wasn't. His fingers were idly rearranging his silverware, his blue eyes glancing at hers restlessly.

She only smiled. "How have things been with you?" she replied, ignoring the question.

He shrugged, acknowledging the slight with that tiny gesture. "With the factory? Well, it could be worse. With me?" he added with a soft laugh. "Life can be lonely."

"Can it?" she asked absently. "I don't have time for loneliness. I'm much too busy."

"Are you staying for good, Keena?" he asked suddenly.

She met his eyes. Along with the cruelty, memories came back of the few good times, of James laughing, teasing her, of the first time he'd kissed her, of long walks in the woods. And then inevitably she recalled that last evening, her initiation into womanhood at his careless hands. . . .

"Goodness, Keena, I've missed you," he said gently, reaching for her hand. Smiling, he caressed it slowly.

Don't fall for it, she told herself firmly. *Don't listen.* But the pull of the past was strong, and James was handsome, and she was falling ever so gently under his spell. More by the minute.

"I've . . . missed you too," she replied hesitantly.

The waiter, standing patiently with his tray, finally caught James's eye and began to serve the oysters Rockefeller that James had ordered along with a magnificent salad, filet of sole, and dainty little croissants with butter.

James cleared his throat, his long face betraying his obvious interest in Keena to an outsider. Keena looked up from her salad, her eyes wary as they searched his intent face. He was looking at her in a new and exciting way. She smiled at him. The evening was suddenly full of promise.

"After we leave here," James murmured sensuously, "how would you like to drive over to the lake?"

That had been one of their favorite haunts years ago when he took her out. Her eyes involuntarily sought his mouth. He had nice lips. Almost too soft to be a man's, and she remembered the faintly chaste feel of them. She wondered if he'd learned to be more patient with women. Involuntarily, her mind went back to the way Nicholas had kissed her in the Rolls, and she flushed suddenly.

James, thinking the blush was due to the question he'd asked her about the moonlight drive along the lake, smiled confidently.

"How about it?" he murmured over his wineglass.

"Uh—" she began.

"Excuse me, sir," the waiter interrupted delicately, "there's a call for you."

James muttered under his breath as he got to his feet. "Excuse me, darling?" he asked possessively.

Darling! "Of course," she murmured breathlessly.

Her eyes followed him to the phone at the desk. She studied his long, elegant back while he spoke into the receiver, made a sharp gesture, and hung up. His face was troubled when he came back to the table.

"We'll have to leave, I'm afraid," he muttered, pausing long enough to take one last sip of wine before he helped Keena out of her chair. "I can't tell you how sorry I am. I'll drop you off on my way to the plant."

"What's wrong?" she asked.

"There's been some problem at the plant," he sighed. "Strange, I don't remember my night watchman having a cold, but I suppose the line could have been bad."

She thought about that on the way out. "Did he have an unusually deep voice, you mean?" she asked with dawning curiosity.

"Deeper than normal," he replied absently. He paused to pay the check. "That company has been nothing but a headache to me since the day my father died. There are times when I wish . . ." He shrugged. "Never mind. Maybe it's fate. An albatross around my neck to curse me." He smiled down at her. "And maybe a beautiful fairy can break the spell."

She smiled back as she followed him out to his car. All the way home she thought about that strange phone call. She didn't mention her suspicions to James, but she had a sneaking hunch that he wasn't going to find any trouble at his plant at all.

James pulled up at the steps behind the elegant Rolls-Royce.

"How about tomorrow night? Oh, damn, no, I've got a business meeting with a client in Atlanta. Thursday, for dinner?" he asked with flattering eagerness.

"I'd like that," she agreed.

"Sorry about this," he murmured, leaning toward her. But a second before he could kiss her, the front porch light blazed on and James drew back abruptly.

He cleared his throat. "Well, good night," he said reluctantly.

"Good night," Keena replied, forcing herself not to explode with the rage she was feeling. When she got inside that house, she was going to shoot Nicholas Coleman!

"Is he staying more than a day?" James added, nodding toward the Rolls with a distasteful look.

"No," she said firmly. She got out of the car and waved him off. When she turned toward the house, there was fury in every slender line of her body.

She took the steps two at a time and blazed through the front door, her dark hair curling softly around her face like a halo, her green eyes glittering with anger.

Mandy turned from the door into her own quarters at the foot of the staircase, her eyebrows raised. "Home so early?" she asked.

Keena glared at her. "Did Nicholas make any phone calls tonight?"

"He always makes a lot of phone calls," Mandy replied smoothly. "I'm sorry about the porch light," she added sheepishly. "I thought I heard a car, and it didn't occur to me that it would be you so soon . . ."

Keena waved the apology off. "Where's Nicholas?"

"Upstairs, I guess. I heard water running a minute or so ago."

"Getting ready for bed, no doubt," Keena growled, tossing her coat and purse onto a chair in the hall before she stalked up the staircase. "He is not getting away with this. I will not have my life controlled by that . . . that tyrant!"

Mandy only grinned as she went into her room.

Keena marched up the steps to the room Nicholas had commandeered and, without thinking, threw open the door and walked in.

The first thing that caught her eye was Nicholas. He was standing in front of his chest of drawers combing his dark, still-damp hair into place. The second thing that caught her eye was the fact that he didn't have a stitch of clothing on his powerful, dark, hair-covered body.

Four

Keena froze just inside the door she'd slammed behind her, gaping at him involuntarily.

He lifted a dark eyebrow, as unconscious of his nudity as a stag in the forest. "Do come in," he murmured with a half smile. He laid down the comb and picked up his electric razor. "That bathroom stays fogged up forever," he commented. He lifted the humming razor to his chin. "I have to do this twice a day or I wouldn't be able to get it off with sandpaper. Sit down and tell me about your date."

"Uh . . ." she began, her breath catching in her throat. She wasn't totally innocent. But the looks of a man had never quite affected her this way, and she couldn't tear her eyes away from Nicholas. It had never occurred to her that a man could be called beautiful, but he was, his big, muscular body, perfectly sculpted, without a single curve or angle in excess.

He glanced at her, patient amusement on his face. "If I'm not embarrassed, why should you be?" he asked. "Sit down. You're perfectly safe."

She moved numbly to a chair against the wall and eased down into it. "I . . . just wanted to ask you a question," she stammered.

He shifted, raising one cheek toward the mirror as he drew the shaver over it. "What?"

"Did . . . did you call the restaurant and tell James there was a problem at his company?" she asked point blank.

The shaver hummed in mid-air as he turned and stared at her. "What restaurant did you go to?" he asked politely.

She fought a losing battle to keep her eyes

on his face, and he laughed softly at the color that blazed in her softly rouged cheeks.

"You blush delightfully, did you know? Surely you must have guessed at some point in our relationship that I was a man."

She nodded. "But . . . I . . . that is . . ."

"My God, you're repressed," he sighed. "I really will have to take you to a blue movie."

She let a smile peek from her lips. "I don't need to go anymore," she murmured.

He chuckled, turning back to the mirror. He drew the razor across his square jaw and under his chin. "You should be properly flattered that I haven't grabbed for a robe," he said with a mischievous glance as he finished and turned off the razor, running a hand over the newly shaven areas to check for missed spots. "At my age, I'm damned particular about being seen like this."

"Even by women?" she blurted out.

He looked across the room at her, a long, intense look that made her pulse race. "It depends on the woman," he replied.

"You . . . don't mind me," she murmured, confused.

"No."

Involuntarily, her eyes roved over his body, lingering curiously, memorizing, trembling inwardly at the sheer sensuality of it, the blatant power in those bronze, hair-covered muscles.

"So, do you approve?" he asked very quietly.

She averted her eyes suddenly, embarrassed by her fascination with the sight of him. "I'm sorry. I didn't mean to stare."

"And I've already told you, I don't mind." He moved toward her, a slow movement she caught out of the corner of her eye. Uncharacteristically, she jumped and rose from the chair with a start, tension in the soft lines of her body.

He stopped, froze in place, and she'd never seen that particular look on a man's face before—desire shadowed with smothered anger.

"If it's that much of a damned trauma, go to bed," he said harshly, turning back to the chest of drawers. He took a short terry-cloth robe from a drawer and shouldered into its thick brown softness, jerking the sash together with sharp, deft movements.

"I'm sorry," she said, wary of his gunpowder temper. "Nicholas, I didn't mean to do that, I . . . well, I . . . damn it, what did you expect? This isn't exactly our usual style of conversing."

"Forget it." He picked up the comb and ran it through his hair, his face still dark and taut.

She stood there, helpless, her hands twisting

the elegant velvet of her long skirt. "Nick . . ." she murmured pleadingly.

"Go to bed, Keena," he repeated, his voice rigid.

"How can I, when you're furious with me?" she burst out. "I panicked. All right! For heaven's sake, I'm lucky I didn't go right out the window!"

That seemed to calm him. One corner of his mouth turned up. He chuckled softly. "You're on the second story," he reminded her.

"That first step would be a doozy, wouldn't it?" she teased.

He lifted his shoulders. "I overreacted. I'm damned touchy."

She was just beginning to realize what he meant. She knew men were sensitive about such things, but the degree of Nick's sensitivity hadn't occurred to her until now.

"About what?" she asked gently. "Nicholas, you must know that you're magnificent."

He darted a glance at her. "Compared to whom?"

She glared at him. "You might be surprised," she said haughtily.

"Liar." He laid down the comb and stuck his big hands into the pockets of the robe. "You may not be a vestal virgin, honey, but I'm damned sure that you haven't much of a scrapbook to compare me with. Was it always in the dark?" he added with a veil of humor over a rather harsh curiosity.

She knew what he was asking, but she wasn't about to give him the satisfaction of an answer. He didn't know all of the truth about herself and James and she was reluctant to tell him how foolish she had been.

"You never did answer me," she said, changing the subject. "And you haven't asked why I'm home so early."

He blinked. "Would you like to run that by me one more time?"

She sighed. "Don't you want to know why I'm not still out with James?"

"Harris wouldn't be stupid enough to take you along to the plant if there were trouble," he replied dryly.

"Aha!" she burst out. "You did make that phone call!"

"I was bored," he said with a careless shrug. "There isn't a lot to do here." He glanced around the room. "I could paint the door facings, I suppose."

"You could go back to New York," she suggested.

"I'm taking a vacation. I work hard."

"I realize that, but couldn't you take your vacation in Acapulco or Martinique or Paris?"

"I like it here," he said.

"Nicholas!" She stamped her small foot. "Have you thought about the gossip it's going to cause if you stay here? James is already upset."

"Is he?" he purred. "How disappointing."

"You're fouling up all my plans," she grumbled, her eyes spitting fire at him.

"You're not doing mine a hell of a lot of good either," he replied, his broad face harder than she'd seen it in weeks.

"I am not, repeat *not*, going back to New York until I've renovated this house and given my party," she pouted. "Put that in your pipe and smoke it!"

"I don't smoke a pipe," he pointed out.

She shifted restlessly. "What do you want?" she moaned. "What are you trying to do, Nicholas?"

"Maybe I'm trying to get you to stop running from me, have you ever thought about that?" he asked thoughtfully.

She gaped at him. "But I've never run from you," she protested.

He searched her face with slow, darkening eyes. "Honey, you've done little else since the day we met. You'll let me just so close before you start backing away."

"Do I?"

He turned away, reaching for his cigarettes and lighter. He lit up before he turned back, blowing out a thin cloud of smoke. "What are you afraid of, Keena? Is sex such an ordeal for you that you've given it up, or are you afraid that I'd be too rough with you? Despite the way you seem to have a knack for making my temper boil, Keena, believe me, I'm not an impatient lover."

"I'm not . . . not afraid of you like that," she replied. The conversation was getting rapidly out of hand. "Don't rush me, Nicholas."

"Rush you, for God's sake!" he ground out, his dark eyes splintering. "It's been six years!"

"The world is full of women," she growled, feeling a surge of sheer fury as she remembered his mistress. "If all you need is to satisfy a passing urge, I'm sure you could pick up someone in town."

He looked as if she'd slapped him in the face, and for just an instant he tensed, as if he were considering retaliation. She tensed, too, ready to run at the first movement of that tall, overpowering form. But all at once the tension seemed to drain out of him. He turned around and moved to the bed, pausing to pick up the white alarm clock and set it.

"We've been friends for a long time," he said quietly. "I thought you knew me well enough to realize that I could *never* think of you that way."

She felt shame like a fog surrounding her, and she had the grace to flush. "I didn't mean that," she told him. "Nick, I don't know what's wrong with me tonight, I haven't meant half of what I've said. I just . . . I think I'm rattled, that's all," she finished, and ran a smoothing hand over her hair. "Don't hate me."

"That's not likely." He unfastened the robe and threw it on a chair, throwing back the covers to ease himself under them. The sheet and coverlet covered him to the waist, leaving his broad, hair-rough chest and muscular arms bare. "Turn out the light on your way out, will you, honey?" He yawned. "God, I'm tired."

She studied him lying there, so strong and imposing, and she wanted more than anything to climb into bed with him and be held and soothed and comforted. It had been a horrible day and the time she'd been away from him had dragged on forever. And now here he was and all she could do was scream at him. James Harris, the party, revenge, all of it took a backseat to the things she'd said to Nicholas tonight, and she hated herself for every single one of them.

"Nick . . ." she whispered, her lips trembling, her eyes misting with unshed tears.

He studied her sad little face across the room, and suddenly held out his arms. "Come here, little fox," he said deeply.

She all but ran to him, hurting with all the pent-up emotions of a lifetime, like a little wounded thing seeking a gentle hand.

He pulled her down beside him, with the cover between them, and held her close and warm in his bare arms. Under her moist cheek she could feel the crisp dark hair and warm muscles. She could smell soap and cologne mingling with the scent of the man himself and she'd never felt so safe, so utterly safe.

"I've been horrible, haven't I?" she whimpered softly. Her small fist collided gently with his chest. "Oh, Nick, what's the matter with me?" she wailed.

"The shell's cracking loose, that's all," he murmured comfortingly, one big hand idly caressing on her back through the softness of the velvet.

"Shell?"

"The one you've worn around you for the past six years," he explained. "There have been men in your life, but even if you've been with them physically, you've managed somehow to remain untouched emotionally."

She opened her eyes and stared across his broad chest to the chair against the wall. "Nick . . ."

"Hmmm?" he murmured.

She licked her lips, hesitating over the question.

He tugged at a short lock of hair. "There's nothing you can't ask me. What is it?"

"Would it matter if I'd been with other men?"

"To me?" he asked casually. "No. Why?"

She couldn't explain the question to herself, much less to him. It had been important to know the answer, despite the fact that there had been only one man in her life in any intimate sense.

"You're very quiet all of a sudden," he commented, his voice tender in the silence of the room.

She raised her head and propped herself up beside him, her fingers idly tracing patterns in the rough hair on his chest.

"I can't figure you out," she replied gently. Her eyes searched his, looking but not finding anything out of the ordinary in them. Only a slight dilation of the pupils disclosed any emotion at all.

"What do you want to know?" he asked.

"Nick, do you want me?" She put it into

words, whispered it as if it were something secret.

His fingers caught hers and stilled them on his chest, warming them. "What a hell of a question!" He chuckled softly, sounding more like the friend he'd always been than like a lover.

"Do you?" she persisted, frowning.

He drew in a deep, slow breath. "I'd rather not go into that right now," he told her. "It's late, and I'm bone tired."

"Too tired to answer a single question?" she teased, half-irritated.

He lifted an eyebrow. "Miss Whitman," he said deeply, "I could answer that particular question without a single word, and in a way that would shock your uninitiated soul." He chuckled wickedly at the starburst of color that drowned out her peaches-and-cream complexion. "I see you understand me. Now, if you're through with inane questions, would you like to leave me in peace and let me get some sleep? The feel of you is, quite frankly, disturbing me."

She couldn't smother a laugh. "Complaints, complaints," she teased delightedly, pleased for some hidden reason that he felt more than comradeship for her, that she could disturb him.

"Would you like to take off your dress and discuss it?" he asked with narrowing eyes.

"Why would I have to take off my dress?" she asked in mock innocence as she got to her feet and smoothed the wrinkled velvet down over her full hips.

"You're tempting fate, foxy lady," he murmured as he rolled over onto his back and stared up at her.

Her eyes searched his with all the brief humor gone out of them. "Would it be so terrible if I let you make love to me?" she asked quietly.

"For a woman who backs away from me constantly, you're suddenly damned brave," he murmured.

She stared down at her feet. "I'm confused."

"I know that. But confusion is no good foundation for a love affair," he said bluntly. "Get Harris out of your system before you make me any offers, Keena," he added with a faintly dangerous note in his voice. "It's all or nothing with me—in everything."

She didn't know whether to be insulted or flattered, and her own boldness shocked her. She'd never been that forward with any man.

"You don't understand about James," she began quietly.

"No?" He studied her slender figure with a

practiced eye. "I understand you better than you think. You don't have to prove anything to anyone, Keena. You've made your mark in the world. But something in you needs to see the past acknowledge that success. And for the past, we might as well say James Harris." He flexed his shoulders against the pillow. "Play your games, honey. But don't expect any cooperation from me. I won't be a stand-in for another man."

"How dare you!" she spat out.

"Do you want me?" he asked curtly.

She opened her mouth to speak, but the words trapped themselves in her throat. Want him? Of course she wanted him, but the question was, how?

"When you can answer me without any hesitation, we'll have a nice long talk," he said gently. "Now get out of here and let me sleep."

"With pleasure," she ground out, storming to the door.

"Keena!"

She stared at the doorknob in her hand. "Yes?"

"Have you ever considered that maybe the only reason you think you want Harris is because you couldn't get him?"

She opened the door quietly, but she slammed it furiously behind her.

A WAITING GAME

* * *

Mandy seemed to sense something at breakfast the next morning. The house was uncannily quiet before the arrival of the painters, who had promised to be through by today, and Keena and Nicholas were quiet as well.

She glanced at him once and read patient, faint amusement in his dark eyes as they dropped deliberately to the soft swell of her breasts under the yellow sweater she was wearing with her hacking jacket and jodhpurs.

Mandy went to get the coffeepot for refills when they finished the scrambled eggs, country ham, and homemade biscuits, and Nicholas laughed softly at the expression on Keena's face.

He leaned back in his chair like a well-fed lion. His shaggy mane of dark hair was slightly ruffled; his eyes were a little bloodshot. But in a red shirt that emphasized his darkness and the dark slacks that hugged, lovingly, every powerful line of his legs, she was hard-pressed to find fault with him.

"You've barely said two words to me this morning," he observed, relaxing in the chair like a man who'd found a new hobby and was preparing to enjoy it to the fullest.

"What would you like?" she asked with

sweet politeness, "the Gettysburg Address or a soliliquy from *Hamlet*?"

"How about a chorus of 'I Love You, Truly'?" he murmured.

She fought the color but lost to its quick invasion of her face.

"I didn't," she replied tightly.

"Didn't what?"

"Love you, truly—or *otherwise.*"

"Have you become too blasé for love, little fox?" he asked quietly.

She toyed with her empty cup. "Love is just a synonym for infatuation," she said bitterly. "I had my heart stepped on enough to last me a lifetime. I suppose I expected too much from men."

"Such as?"

"Loyalty," she replied. "Courtesy, kindness, consideration . . ."

"Buy a dog," he suggested.

She glared at him. "You have no poetry in your soul."

"Perhaps not. I'm a realist."

"What do you expect from your women?" she tossed back.

Something flared in his dark eyes at the undisguised sarcasm in her tone. He slammed his napkin down onto the table and stood up.

"Raw sex, of course," he said with biting sarcasm. "When I want it, however the hell I want it."

She glared up at him with her lower lip faintly tremulous. She didn't really want to argue with him, but lately they set each other off with every other sentence. It was new and disturbing to fight with Nicholas. She wasn't at all sure she liked it. She missed the old, easy relationship with its comforting aspects. There was nothing comforting about the icy stranger beside the table. He looked more than a little dangerous.

Mandy came through the door with the coffeepot before Keena could get the words off her tongue, and her sharp eyes didn't miss much.

"Isn't it a little early in the morning for war games?" she asked the taciturn man, with a grin.

"Tell Madame Attila," Nicholas growled, turning on his heel to leave the room.

Keena stood up, her face stormy, her eyes stinging with sudden tears. "I'm going for a ride," she said tightly. "I'll be back later."

Mandy looked after them, then at the coffeepot. She shrugged and poured herself a cup before she sank down in the chair and leaned back to drink it.

* * *

The woods were lovely and quiet, except for the whisper of the pines high above, and Keena felt the rage burn out of her in the peace of it all. Nicholas had only been baiting her, but she was still shaking from the encounter. He could look so fierce when he was angry, and she was hurt by the way he'd glared at her. She never should have taunted him, but she couldn't help herself.

She settled lower in the saddle, finding peace in the creak of the rich saddle leather, the measured thud of the horse's hooves on the hard pine-straw–covered forest floor. It was a glorious day, all blue, and fluffy, with sculptured clouds and a cutting February wind. The little brown mare wasn't a purebred, but Keena liked her. She was gaited, barely four years old, with a touch of mischief mixed in with her gentle nature. It was fun riding her. She thought about Nicholas riding a horse and laughed involuntarily, momentarily forgetting the argument. She could visualize him only on some towering black stallion. He'd look ridiculous on anything less.

A noise nearby startled her. She pulled back on the reins and turned in time to see James riding through an opening in the thick underbrush. She smiled, delighted at the unexpected meeting.

He looked trendy in his hacking jacket and jodhpurs, his booted feet firm in the stirrups and an Irish walking hat atop his head. His blue eyes twinkled merrily.

"I called the house," he told her, reining in beside her on the wide trail. "Mandy said I'd find you here."

"Did she?" she murmured, and her eyes flirted with his. She felt reckless this morning.

"With a little persuasion," he admitted. He studied her slender figure approvingly. "You look good."

"Thanks. So do you." She peeked at him from under her lashes. "Did you settle your problem last night?"

His face clouded. "It was a crank call," he grumbled. "I went rushing over there only to find that my night watchman was as surprised as I was. He hadn't made the call. Can you imagine anyone with such a bad sense of humor?"

"Oh, no," she agreed readily. It cost her an effort not to burst out laughing. She shouldn't have been amused, but Nicholas could be such a devil . . .

"No harm done, I suppose," he sighed. His eyes twinkled. "Care to ride along with me for a bit? I've got a meeting later in the morning, but I'd enjoy the company. I'm going down to the river and back."

"I'd love to," she agreed, letting the mare fall into step beside his gelding.

She couldn't help but remember how many times in her youth she'd haunted these woods for just a glimpse of James on his horse. Her heart had been such a fragile thing in those long-ago days, and she'd wanted so badly to give it to him. But she was older now, wary of emotions. She enjoyed James's company, but she didn't want to risk getting involved with him again. She knew from painful experience how devastating that could be. She wasn't really tempted, she realized, to give James any second chances.

Involuntarily, her mind went back to Nicholas, to the way she'd seen him last night, and her mind went into chaos. She'd never seen anything as devastating as Nicholas without clothes. Her dreams had been wild ones, adding to her irritable mood this morning when she'd made that unforgivable remark about his women. But when she thought about women, she thought about Maria, and the certainty that she'd seen Nicholas in every way there was only made her more furious. She just couldn't bear the thought of him touching any other woman.

"You're very quiet." James interrupted her thoughts as they reached the banks of the wide, softly running river.

"It's peaceful here," she replied. "I'm not used to peace. I live at a breakneck pace these days."

He saw an opening and took it. "You must be very successful."

She nodded. "I design for an exclusive clientele in addition to my leisure line."

"Do you have your own manufacturing company as well?" he persisted.

"Nicholas and I have an arrangement about that," she replied. "I contract my big cuts out to him, although I have a small cutting room and sample sewers. Nicholas owns a number of textile mills and manufacturing companies," she added.

"I know. Do you, uh, suppose he might be interested in acquiring another one?" he asked, suddenly serious as his blue eyes met hers.

She studied him warily. "Thinking of selling yours?" she asked.

"I'm playing around with the idea," he admitted. "Could you, uh, mention it to Coleman?"

If we ever speak again, she thought silently, but she smiled half-heartedly. Was this what he'd been up to all along with his sudden interest in her? She felt used, and not a little let down. It was old times again.

"Yes, I could mention it to him," she laughed shortly. "Shall I have him call you?"

"Please." His face lit up like a blazing candle. He got down from his mount and reached up to lift Keena down beside him, his chest lightly touching hers. "You're a lovely thing," he murmured.

"Useful, too," she commented dryly. He was so easy to see through. Nothing like Nicholas, who was a closed book.

He grimaced. "It sounded that way, I suppose," he admitted. His eyes searched hers. "But I am . . . interested in you."

"Why shouldn't you be?" she asked, slinging a bitter smile up at him. "After all, I'm rich, halfway famous, and I have useful contacts."

He scowled. She puzzled him. She was nothing like what he'd expected. He'd imagined he could wind her around his little finger, but it was she who was doing the winding, and he didn't like it.

"You're twisting my words," he said coolly. "I didn't mean it that way."

"No?" she purred with faint hostility. *Damn all men everywhere.* "How did you mean it, then, James, dear?"

"You little cat . . ." He bent suddenly to take her mouth.

His mouth was firm and warm, and he was making no concessions at all. It was a lover's kiss that the eighteen-year-old girl who'd worshipped him would have swooned from. But Keena was years older, and she had Nicholas's ardor for comparison. James was practiced, that much was obvious. He knew how to use his experience, exploring her mouth to the fullest. But Keena wasn't giving him the response he expected. It made him rough, until she pushed at his chest.

He drew back, breathing heavily, his emotions obviously on the verge of loss of control. His fingers bit into her upper arms.

"You don't give an inch, do you?" he asked curtly, glaring down at her.

"What did you expect me to do, swoon?" she asked half-angrily. "I'm hardly eighteen anymore."

"Good God, I know that," he ground out, lowering his eyes to her high breasts. "I've always wanted you, even nine years ago."

"Wanted, yes," she agreed. "But desire, without any deeper emotion to give it meaning, is rather empty."

He relaxed his grip a little. "I don't know very much about deep emotions," he admitted quietly. "I like women. I like variety. I don't really care for emotional involvement. Not at all."

"Neither do I," she replied, and that seemed to irritate him, as if he had nothing to give, but still expected to receive in full measure.

"You might change your mind," he murmured. He bent again. "Let's try that again."

She let him kiss her, but the earthshaking passion she'd once felt for him had been reduced to a faint tremor of remembrance that worked its way down her body and seemed to drain out of her. That irritated her, and she clung closer, trying to force it.

He wrapped her up against him, gentle now, very ardent, but behind the practiced lover there was only remembered bitterness. Her heart, expecting a banquet, had come away with crumbs.

He moved away finally, his eyes dancing. "Not bad," he murmured. "We'll have to practice more though."

She let him keep his illusions with a smile and a tiny shrug that could have meant anything. "I have to get back," she said.

"Have dinner with me tomorrow night, as we planned?" he asked, and for an instant there really was something new in his voice. "I

wish I didn't have this meeting in Atlanta today . . ."

"Tomorrow will give me something to look
forward to," she told him.

She'd wanted to let him sweat for a few
days, to build his interest and then . . . But
she was just beginning to sense that there
might be a man under that mask James wore,
and she was curious about what was really behind it. But Nick wasn't going to like it. She
knew that before she waved good-bye to
James and headed the little more back toward
the house.

There were so many everyday problems in
her life lately, she sighed. Nicholas, being suddenly possessive and irritable and impossible,
and James, just turning into a person she
might really like.

Nicholas was the biggest puzzle she faced.
He'd never been overly concerned about her,
except that he kept a watchful eye over her
dates to make sure she wasn't in danger from
them. But about James he was being positively
unreasonable. What did he want? Not her
body, she remembered with embarrassment,
or he wouldn't have hesitated to take what
she'd offered him so blatantly last night. His
rejection had hurt more than she'd realized at
the time. She could disturb him all right, but

not to any overpowering extent. And there was no moral reason for him to hold back since she had been so willing. What kind of game was he playing? Was he just being protective, not wanting to see James hurt her?

By the time she got back to the house, the only thing she was sure of was that she wished she'd never come back to Georgia. If only her father were still alive, to listen to her problems, to advise her. She missed him so. At least her battle with Nicholas had helped her over the grief. It was hard to be sad when your temper was being constantly pushed to the boiling point.

She walked into the house only to find Nicholas pacing the hall. He whirled when he saw her.

"So there you are," he growled. "Come in here."

She puffed up proudly, glaring at the broad back going into the study. "Nicholas . . ."

"We don't have a lot of time," he returned, his face solemn, and she felt a surge of apprehension as she followed him quickly into the room.

"What is it?" she asked.

He rammed his hands in his pockets. With his back to the light coming in through the window, he had a faintly ominous shadow around him.

"There's no easy way to say it," he said quietly. "There's been a fire at your office, Keena. Almost everything you'd done for your fall line has been destroyed."

Five

Her mind seemed to go numb at the words. She stared at him. "A fire?" she echoed.

"That's right. Do you want to sit down?"

She shook her head. Her eyes went wild. "But I've still got orders to fill," she burst out. "The last of the summer line is still being sewn, and we'd just received the cloth for the fall-and-winter line and the samples were ready for the boutiques!"

"Don't panic!" he shot at her. "Now just calm

down. How long will it take you to replace the specs and the spring collection designs?"

She felt herself trembling. She moved jerkily, uncertainly. "I . . . I'm not sure. They, uh, they had some innovations . . ."

He moved toward her, easing her down on the sofa. He knelt in front of her and drew her head onto his shoulder. His big fingers soothed the back of her neck gently.

"I'm here," he said quietly. "It's all right. I'm here. There's nothing to be afraid of."

Tears trickled from her closed eyes, hot and salty, flowing down into the corner of her mouth. All that work, gone! How many of those designs would she be able to remember? Why hadn't she moved the portfolio of the spring fashions to her apartment? Why hadn't she left them in the office at Nicholas's plant? And what about the bulk orders on the fall line that the cutting room had just received the fabric for? Bolts of cloth, expensive cloth, all gone. And the summer boutique orders that had just been completed? Were they gone as well?

Her fingers crept around his neck and she clung to him, comforted by his very size.

"Why?" she whimpered.

"There's always a reason, honey," he replied

quietly. "I've learned that, if nothing else. Just chalk it up to fate and go on from there."

"How can I go on?" she wailed. "With what?"

"Sheer grit, if that's what it takes."

"Hold me tight," she whispered, inching closer.

"Much closer than this, and I'll crack a rib," he said with a whisper of humor in his deep voice. He got to his feet, melting her body into the hard contours of his until she felt the imprint of him all the way to her toes.

"Oh, Nick, I'm so glad you're here," she whispered.

"You weren't when you went out the door," he recalled.

"Not now," she pleaded. "Don't let's fight. I'm not up to it."

He rocked her against him, soothing her. "What is it about my women that sets you off, Keena?" he asked in a deep, soft tone. "That wasn't the first time you made some offhanded remark about them."

This was getting dangerous. She shrugged. "Did I? I haven't done it intentionally."

"Perhaps you didn't realize it," he replied.

She looked up into his eyes through the mist of tears, and it was as if she'd never really seen him before. Her eyes traced the broad, hard lines of his face, his straight nose, his deep-set dark eyes, the sensuous line of his mouth, his jaw square as a tracker after signs of his quarry. Her eyes met his again suddenly, and a wild, explosive chill ran through her, a tingle of pleasure that was devastating.

"Your legs are trembling," he murmured quietly.

They were. Rubbery, unsupportive, and she was too shocked by her new discovery to explain it.

"Did he kiss you?" he asked suddenly, with hard, narrowed eyes.

She nodded, her gaze locked into his.

His cool eyes went to her soft mouth. "Was it good?" he persisted.

Her breath caught just under her breasts and refused to submerge. "It . . . was pleasant," she corrected.

"Is that what you feel when I kiss you— pleasant?" he whispered as his dark head bent.

"Nick . . . the fire . . ." she managed weakly.

"People should always do wild things in times of disaster, honey," he murmured as his mouth broke against hers. "Didn't you know? Put your arms around my waist and hold on."

She obeyed him without a murmur, her mouth accepting his, inviting his tongue, his teeth, feeling his body intimately against hers with a wild surge of pleasure that made her moan.

"Volcanic," he whispered into her open mouth. "My God, you quake all over when I take your mouth. Feel me, Keena, feel the tensing that happens when I hold you. Is it like this with him? Is he even capable of passion?"

Her short nails were digging madly into his muscular back; her body was pressing as close as it could get to his, savoring the rough, warm contact with those steely muscles. She barely heard him, her mouth accepting his, begging for more, drowning in the sweet, hard crush of it, the intimate thrusting of his tongue, the nip of his strong white teeth.

His hands ran up her sides, almost but not quite intimate in their exploration. "Answer me," he murmured gruffly.

"I go . . . crazy . . . when you kiss me," she whispered brokenly, her eyes riveted to his hard mouth. "Nick, don't stop."

"It's now or never, little fox," he murmured, dropping one last hard kiss on her mouth before he raised his head with a sharp, rough sigh. His eyes were stormy, his chest rising and falling as unevenly as hers.

She hit his chest with her hand, feeling the

softness of the red fabric under her fingers.
"Nick!"

"I can't take you on the floor," he whispered,
mischief in his dark eyes.

Her face blossomed with color and she hid
it against him.

"Business first, little one," he murmured,
holding her gently. "I've got to fly up to New
York today. You might as well come with me
in the jet."

"You brought it here?" she murmured daz-
edly.

"Where in hell would I park it, in the rose
garden?" he asked with a short laugh. "I had
Mark Segars fly it down this morning. It's
waiting at the airport."

"I'd better pack then," she murmured,
dreading the trip, dreading the sight of her elegant office all black and charred, all the burnt
remains of that gorgeous fabric. "Nick, did
they salvage anything?"

"Ann grabbed up a handful of sketches just
before the curtains caught," he replied. "And a
few samples. But by the time the firemen got
there, it was far too late. They managed to
save the rest of the building, but your office,
the cutting room, and the shipping room are
gone, along with every scrap of fabric in the
place."

She nodded. This must be how it felt to lose an arm—this lonely, empty feeling in the pit of her stomach. But the arm she'd lost was her livelihood, and she had to find some way to replace it. Thank God she could still count on Nicholas. She looked up at him helplessly.

"Go on," he said, nudging her toward the door. "It will be all right. Trust me."

"Haven't I always?" she asked gently.

He nodded. "Too much sometimes," he said dryly, watching her eyes fall quickly.

She hurried out the door.

Two hours later they were well on the way to New York in Nicholas's private jet. She sat lost in her worries, her hand clinging like glue to Nicholas's big, warm one. He seemed to like that contact, because he didn't make a move to break it, even when he smoked or drank his coffee. His own fingers were comforting, but vaguely caressing, as if he enjoyed having her cling to him. Funny, she thought through the nightmare of reality, he didn't seem the kind of man who'd enjoy a clinging woman.

"I hope Mandy can manage while I'm gone," she murmured. "I hated leaving her behind."

"She'll have everything organized by the time you get back," he told her.

"I know." She leaned her head against his

broad shoulder. "Oh, Nick, I'm so glad you're with me. I don't think I could face it alone."

"I like looking after you, Miss Independence," he murmured against her hair. "When you let me, that is. I wish to God you'd let me know about your father."

"You were busy," she sighed.

"I'm never, not now or ever, too busy when you need me," he said shortly. "Will you jot down a memo to that effect and promise to read it at least twice a week?"

She smiled wearily. "I'll try." She peeked up at him. "Nick, why are you so good to me?" she asked seriously. "You always have been, and I know it isn't because you feel paternal or because you want me."

He searched her eyes quietly. "I want you, all right," he replied in a deep, slow tone. "And you damned well know it."

She swallowed. "Not to the exclusion of everything else."

"Are you sure about that?" he asked.

Her eyes went down to the gray and burgundy patterned tie and his white silk shirt. "You always manage to push me away in time," she said under her breath, feeling the rejection all over again.

"With good reason," he reminded her.

She jerked her eyes up to his. "James?" she asked with a bitter smile.

His eyes searched hers. "Not entirely."

She shifted and let her face slide down against his soft, warm shirtfront once more. "You're worse than any clam, Nicholas."

"With you, I have to be. Go to sleep, tired little girl. I'll take care of you."

He would too. She felt her eyes mist over before she let the drowsiness and emotional turmoil lapse into sleep. It had been a long time since anyone had cared enough to worry about her.

They stopped by Keena's apartment, Jimson effortlessly steering the Rolls through the rush-hour traffic to the Manhattan high-rise apartment complex she called home.

She felt like a stranger in the elegant confines, replete with white curtains and carpeting and chrome and blue-velvet upholstered furniture. It seemed artificial, somehow, after the big, rambling old house in Ashton and the small-town atmosphere there.

"What's the matter?" Nicholas asked, sensitive to her changed mood.

"Culture shock," she murmured.

He laughed softly. "From rural peace to urban panic in the space of a couple of hours?"

He shook his head. "It's a little worse for me when I come back to this country after a few weeks abroad. Especially on the return trip from the Bahamas. It's the only place on earth where I can really slow down, and then I come home and get slapped in the face with frantic haste."

"I can't picture you ever slowing down," she commented, her eyes ranging all over him. Dressed in a becoming blue business suit, he looked alarmingly conventional for a man who wrote the rules as he went along. It was vaguely unfair, like a wolf wearing wool.

"You're staring, honey," he said quietly.

She drew her eyes away. "Sorry."

"Undressing me mentally?" he murmured wickedly.

She flushed wildly. "Shame on you!"

"You should have committed me to memory, considering the way you studied me that night," he reminded her. "My God, talk about eyes like saucers . . ."

"Nicholas!" she burst out.

"I can't help it," he replied with a strange smile in his dark eyes. "You blush beautifully."

She stared back into his eyes, as if her own were linked to them by a silken cord. He seemed to hold her without moving, to possess her mind as they stared quietly into each other's eyes, and she recalled vividly the feel of his mouth covering hers, the warmth and strength of his body against her. A tingle of pure pleasure made its way through her, and her lips parted on a hungry sigh.

"My God, I want you," he whispered roughly. "We'd better get out of here before I give in to the urge to do something about it."

"That would be a first," she managed, the hunger blatant in her eyes.

"I'm trying to give you time, you little fool," he ground out. "Besides," he laughed shortly, "we can hardly leave Jimson sitting downstairs with the engine running for the next two hours, can we?" he added. "He'd have carbon monoxide poisoning, and where in hell would I find someone to replace him?"

She drew her lips into a nervous smile. Always the humor returned in time to prevent him from letting her inside that hard shell he kept around himself. And she was too shaken to argue.

"What a unique way to go—in a Rolls," she laughed.

"Think of the insurance claims," he replied. "And the loss of Jimson would send me into mourning."

"You might tell him that," she replied as they

started toward the door. "It would make his day."

"Oh, I tell him often enough," he said. He opend the door for her.

She paused just outside it and turned to look up at him. "Nicholas, if I can't meet my commitments, I'll have to close down," she said, letting all her secret fears out into the open.

He reached down and smoothed one broad-tipped finger along her cheekbone. "You won't close down. I'll see to that. Come on, love, let's go and see the damage."

Love. She let him guide her down the hall while a peculiar sensation tickled like a feather around her midriff. Strange how much pleasure the careless endearment gave. Equally strange how quickly she forgot James Harris, pushed everything to the back of her mind but Nicholas's firm grasp on her arm as he led her to the elevator. At the moment, he seemed to comprise her whole world.

Ann Thomson, Keena's dark-haired assistant, was trying to sort out what was left of Keena's designs and spec sheets in the small sample-room office when Keena and Nicholas arrived.

"Oh, you're here!" Ann cried, running to meet her employer. Her slightness made

Keena seem like a giant by comparison. "Darling, what a terrible homecoming," she groaned, embracing the taller woman. "I'm so sorry!"

Keena bit hard on her lip and tried not to cry. "There, there," she murmured, drawing back with a quick swallow and a shake of her head to distribute the tears under her eyelids and keep them from spilling over. "It won't be easy, but we'll pull through. It's just a temporary setback, that's all."

"But all that work," Ann sighed. "All that lovely cloth. And this is all Faye and I managed to salvage." She gestured toward the desk, where a pitiful few sketches, belts, buttons, tops, and one skirt were spread in disarray. The heavy smell of smoke lingered in the air beyond the charred walls, ceiling and floor, and the ashes of the long cutting tables, the huge bales of rolled fabric.

"Cheer up," Nicholas said from behind her, looking imperturbable with his hands in his pockets, his confident expression. "You can borrow any of my people or facilities. And don't worry about this place," he added, dismissing the ruins with a sweep of his big hand. "I'll have the contractors over here first thing in the morning. If you need an office, the two of you can borrow one of mine."

"I can manage here," Ann said, wrinkling her nose, "smoky smell and all." She looked around the sewing room with its two production sewing machines and its racks and desk and drafting table. "Faye and the girls have gone home, but they're coming back first thing in the morning. The worst of it was the cutting room."

"Tell me what fabrics you need and where you buy," Nicholas told Ann. "And I'll have it here by noon tomorrow if I have to buy you the mill that makes it."

"Oh, if you could!" Ann enthused.

"I'll work from my apartment," Keena told them. "Nicholas, if I give you the specs for the small cuts—the ones we did here—could you get me twenty dozen of the dresses and skirts before the end of the week, or would that cripple your own production?"

"I'll manage. Why only twenty dozen?"

"Because they're new styles. I want to send them to a few exclusive boutiques I sell to and see how they go before I risk putting them into mass production. I can give them a trial run before I commit myself to other buyers."

He grinned. "Good economics. You learned early, didn't you?"

She nodded. "I learned all I know from

you," she reminded him. "And you're no novice at it."

"Or at a few other things," he added with a faint gleam in his dark, deep-set eyes.

She laughed under her breath. "How about the cutting-room staff?" she asked the room in general. "Here it is winter, and they're out of work . . ."

"I'll give them jobs until you get back into full production here," Nicholas said, making mincemeat of the problems as quickly as she thought them up. "It's almost March too. Spring's a breath away."

She smiled at that, feeling some of the worry evaporate.

"Now, if there are no other small mountains nagging at your mind, can we go?" he asked. "I've got businesses of my own to groan over."

"I guess that's about all," she sighed. She turned away from the charred cutting room. "Oh, why?" she moaned. "Why now?"

"The firemen said it was the wiring," Ann shrugged. "Anyway, darling, when was there ever a convenient disaster?"

"True, true." Keena gathered up one of her barely used sketchpads and clutched it to her breast. "When Faye comes in, ask her to get me up those prices we discussed when I began work on the spring line, will you, on notions and such? And you know where to find me if you need me."

Ann nodded. She wiped away a tear. "If only I'd been here . . ."

Keena put her arm around her. "I could stand to lose the plant easier than I could bear losing you," she said. "And we were lucky that it was no worse than it is."

Ann shrugged her thin shoulders. "I suppose so. And we are insured."

"Which reminds me . . ." Keena began.

"I'll take care of it," Nicholas said, impatient now, as if the whole thing were beginning to wear on him. "Come on, honey, let's go."

"Yes, your lordship," Keena said, batting her long eyelashes at him.

He narrowed his eyes at her. "Impertinent little thing," he muttered.

"Why, Nicholas, don't blame me. After all, you taught me everything I know," she cooed, waving to Ann as they went out the door.

"Not yet, I haven't," he chuckled.

She tossed him a mischievous smile. "Are you going to?"

"We'll talk about it one of these days," he said. They walked toward the Rolls, feeling the cold wind as the smell of smoke was replaced by that of carbon monoxide from passing traffic. "Right now I've got some knots of my own to untangle. I'll drop you at your apartment on the way to my office."

"Nick, thank you," she said with genuine emotion in her voice as they reached the car. "Maybe I can pay you back someday."

"You owe me nothing, Keena," he said tautly. "Let's go."

He was, she thought, the most confusing man in the world. She was never going to figure him out.

The next week turned into a merry-go-round of days that melted into nights, their dividing line, the presence of either light or darkness outside. Working around the clock, Keena hardly ate, nibbling on fruit and cookies and drinking pots of black coffee. Hour after hour she struggled to fit her memory to the pages of specs that littered the sofa, the coffee table, and the floor, along with figures on the cost of all sorts of accessories, trims, and fabrics.

No one bothered her, as if her coworkers knew that her creativity hit its high peak when she was alone. Only Nicholas invaded her privacy from time to time, bringing in the various Chinese specialties he knew she loved, and other tempting things to stimulate her failing appetite. One morning he showed up at seven o'clock with a full breakfast, which his own excellent chef had prepared, and woke her from a sound sleep on the soft shag carpet to feed her every spoonful himself. He'd charmed her landlady into letting him in with a passkey, and Keena hadn't even been able to work up any indignation over the invasion. It was such a thoughtful act.

"I'm not a baby," she mumbled as Nicholas popped a fresh strawberry into her mouth.

He only smiled, studying her flushed face, her dreamy eyes, and tousled hair with an approving eye. "No," he agreed. "But I think you deserve a little pampering all the same. Eat."

She opened her mouth again and the taste of a warm, flaky croissant joined the last traces of the strawberry.

"Good?" he asked.

She smiled, nodding up at him from her lounging position. "You're so kind to me, Nicholas."

"I have ulterior motives," he assured her, handing her a cup of coffee laced with cream. "I plan to seduce you one night soon, and I'm plying you with good food to get you in the mood."

"How are you going to seduce me if I know about it in advance?" she asked.

His eyes traveled down the olive silk dressing gown fastened around her slender waist, with just a hint of lace from her nightgown peeking out of the low neckline and the parting at the hem. "Oh, I thought I'd wait until you were half asleep and wrestle you down on the rug."

"I'm already on the rug," she pointed out, laying back after she'd replaced her coffee cup on the low table. She smiled. "But I'm much too full to give you my best."

He stretched out beside her, casually dressed for once in a white turtleneck sweater and dark slacks. He looked younger, much more relaxed than usual. She could feel the heat from his body, and her eyes went to his mouth. She ached to have him touch her, kiss her. But he crossed his arms behind his dark, shaggy head and closed his eyes with a musing smile, ignoring her.

"That makes two of us," he murmured. "I ate before I left the house."

She rolled over on her side and studied his profile. "Nicholas, where are you from?" she asked suddenly.

The question seemed to stun him, because it was a full minute before he answered her. "Charleston," he said finally.

"You don't have a Charleston accent," she remarked.

"So I've been told."

"You lived in Atlanta when we met," she reminded him.

"And you never asked if it had always been home. Why the sudden interest?"

She didn't know. She laughed softly. "I was just curious, that's all."

"I keep an apartment in Atlanta now, just as I keep one in Manhattan. But my family goes back to the Revolutionary War in Charleston. One of my ancestors was part of Francis Marion's band, in fact. There's a plantation, complete with huge live oaks, Spanish moss, and the Ashley River running through it all. Rice was the cash crop before the Civil War."

She studied his relaxed face. "Did . . . did you and your wife live there?"

"Misty loved it," he said. "I moved my office to Atlanta after her death. The memories were eating me alive, so I stayed away."

"You were at the office a good bit after that," she recalled.

He smiled, with his eyes still closed. "Until the day I met you, green as grass and shaking with nervous confidence," he chuckled. "When Misty died, there wasn't a person alive I could talk to about it. Everyone was afraid to mention her name around me. Except you."

"You were driving yourself to death," she

said with a sigh. "I figured it was because of grief. Do you still miss her, Nicholas?"

He turned his head and looked at her. "Sometimes. At odd times. Not as much as I used to. You've helped the scars heal."

"I have?" she asked gently.

"You brighten up dark corners in my life," he mused, "when you aren't setting fire to my temper."

She shifted, curling up next to him like a tired kitten next to a warm fire. She settled against his broad chest, fed and safe and comfortable, her cheek on his shoulder, her fingers pressed against the softness of his cashmere sweater. "Talk to me," she murmured. "Tell me about your family. Is there anyone left in Charleston?"

"Nobody worth mentioning. My parents are long dead. Keena, don't do that," he added curtly, stilling the idle fingers making patterns on his chest.

She could feel the effect her nearness was having on him by the sudden rise and fall of his chest. It gave her a sense of power, along with a surge of pure pleasure.

"Killjoy," she murmured. The pressure of the last few days, the lack of food and sleep, were telling on her. She nuzzled closer with a sigh. "Nicholas, I'll have everything caught up tomorrow. I'm going back to Ashton."

He drew in a deep breath, and she felt the muscles under her head stiffen. "For what—Harris?" he growled.

"For me," she returned. She sat up, brushing the hair from her eyes. "Don't ask me to turn around now," she said coolly. "I've made up my mind, and I won't change it."

He glared up at her. "How long do you think I can stay away from my office before things start crumbling around my vice-presidents?" he asked curtly.

"You don't need to go with me," she replied, equally curt.

"Like hell I don't. I'm not handing you over to him," he told her bluntly.

"What if I want to be handed over?" she demanded. She jerked the robe closer around her tense body. "You don't own me."

His eyes sketched every soft curve of her body before they returned to touch on her delicate facial features. "I feel responsible for you," he said finally.

That hurt. Inexplicably, it was a stinging blow.

"Why?" she asked bitterly and with tremulous lips. "Because I could see through the high-powered executive to the man all those years ago? Because I listened when no one else was brave enough to come near you? Thanks for the compliment, *Mr.* Coleman, but don't bother feeling any obligation toward me. I'm quite capable of taking care of myself."

"How do you plan to go about it?" he asked with cold courtesy. "By seducing that second-rate attorney in Ashton?"

Her eyes exploded. "He's not second-rate," she flashed.

He got to his feet with a lithe, graceful movement, and turned away to light a cigarette. "Are you going to marry him?" he asked curtly, glaring at her through a cloud of smoke while he searched the living room for the ashtray she kept for him.

"If I do, what business is it of yours?" she retorted, wounded and wanting to wound.

He stopped in the action of reaching down to flick an ash into the big square ceramic ashtray, his eyes cutting into hers even at the distance. He straightened, towering over the furniture, big and dark and threatening.

"Push just a little harder," he warned in that soft, deep tone that hinted at a hurricane force of anger brewing inside him, "and you'll find out what business of mine it is."

"I'm fairly trembling, Nicholas," she threw at him. She felt reckless as she rarely had in her life, so stung by his opinion of her that she was willing to risk anything, everything. "Is this how you handle your women—with threats?"

The explosion burst into his dark eyes without warning. He tossed his barely touched cigarette into the ashtray and headed straight toward her, retribution in his taut face, in his pantherish stride, in the set of his square jaw.

Six

Her heart lashed against her ribs, but she stood her ground as he moved toward her.

"I'm not afraid of you," she said with bravado, although she felt like crashing through the nearest wall to get away from him.

He didn't bother to answer her. One big arm shot out to jerk her against him while the other went under her knees. He turned, carrying her as if she weighed no more than a sack of groceries, and started down the hall.

"Nicholas—" she began nervously.

"Shut up." He shouldered open the door to her bedroom and strode across the deep blue carpet to toss her onto the rainbow-colored quilt that graced the queen-size bed. He stood beside the bed just long enough to peel off the sweater, baring his broad hair-matted chest, before he came down alongside her.

She tried to get up, but his hands caught her wrists and pressed them down into the soft coverlet over her head. He held her there until her sudden, panicky struggles finally ceased from sheer exhaustion, and she lay breathless, helpless, looking up at him with bright green eyes full of apprehension.

"Not so brave now, are you, little fox?" he asked in a rough, angry tone. His hands slid up to lock her fingers into his, still holding them down on the quilt. His body shifted, so that his chest crushed into her soft breasts and flattened them against it. "Come on, honey, fight me. This is what you've been working up to ever since that night I left for Paris."

She licked her dry lips nervously. "I don't understand."

"Young girls throw rocks at boys, some of them pick fights by calling them names, but it all leads to some kind of physical confrontation," he replied, his eyes stormy even though his voice was calm enough. "You've been trying to goad me into your bed for days. All right, I'm here. Now what are you going to do with me?"

Her lower lip trembled. "You're out of your mind if you think that's what I want," she replied shakily. "Of all the conceited . . ."

He leaned closer, his dark eyes filling the room, his breath warm on her face, his sensuous mouth close enough to brush hers when he spoke. The heat from his body scorched her, and the weight of it was new and pleasant. More than that. Delicious.

He rolled over on his back abruptly, carrying her with him so that he took the weight of her slender body. His hands drew hers to his broad, warm chest, pressing them against the hard hair-covered muscles while he searched her eyes at unnerving closeness.

"Don't mutter insults at me," he whispered deeply. "Besides, this is really all your idea anyway. I'm only following up on your lead, little fox."

His touch was intoxicating. She'd wanted this for a long time, he was right about that. Her hands had itched to run over the muscles of his brawny chest, to test the thickness and crispness of the hair that covered it. But she didn't want to be taken in anger, and she couldn't stand the idea that his feelings were the result of some misplaced sense of responsibility.

"My lead, my eye! If and when I *ever* want you to make love to me—"

His eyes darkened, his jaws tautened. "Right now," he cut in, "I'd settle for turning you over my knee and paddling your charming derrière. My God, you're in an unpleasant mood this morning."

"How do you expect me to be, when you—" She broke off, lowering her eyes to his chest.

"When I what?" he asked quietly. "Come on, don't stop now. When I what?"

"You don't have to . . . to feel *responsible* for me," she said in a tight, wounded tone.

His chest rose and fell slowly. "So that's it." He brushed back the unruly hair from her cheeks. "Don't you like being cared about?"

Her eyes glanced off his and fell again. "I'm not your property. I . . . I don't like being thought of as an obligation—a . . ." She bit her lip as the tears threatened again.

His big, warm fingers caressed her throat idly. "I do what pleases me, Keena," he murmured softly. "That includes taking care of you when you need it. I do nothing out of a sense of obligation. Especially not with you."

She lifted her eyes back to his and searched them, finding nothing more than a patient kind of amusement. "You sounded as if you did. As if you . . . you only came around because you felt you had to."

"I come around," he replied, "because I feel at ease with you. Because I can talk to you. In my position—with my money—it's damned hard to trust people, hasn't that ever occurred to you?"

She studied his nose, focusing on a spot that looked as if someone had broken it once. Unthinking, she reached out and traced the small flaw in its imposing lines.

"I never thought about it, about your money I mean," she admitted. "Nick, how did your nose get broken?"

"In the Navy," he replied. "A slight disagreement over a disciplinary action. Why don't you think about it?"

She shrugged, shifting over him so that her legs were beside his, not being supported by them. "You've been rich ever since I've known you," she explained.

"That's true enough." He studied her face quietly. "You never asked me for anything, even when I knew for a fact that you could just barely pay your rent."

Her eyes opened wide. "How?"

"I was curious about you."

She shifted restlessly. "What else did you find out?"

One corner of his chiseled mouth went up. "That you were too trusting for your own good. I've sweated blood over you, little fox, especially with a couple of your men friends who weren't exactly what I'd call gentlemen."

She laughed. "You did a thorough job of discouraging one in particular," she murmured humorously, remembering the coworker whose jaw Nicholas had broken.

He sighed wearily. "I owe three of these gray hairs to you."

"Which ones?" She tugged at one silver hair among the dark, curling ones on his broad chest. "This one?"

"Among others." His fingers bit into the small of her back. "Keena, I want to make love to you."

Her eyes flickered against the wildness that was smoldering in his. She seemed to stop breathing, the tension thinned so between them.

"You . . . you didn't the other night," she whispered uncertainly.

"You were afraid of me," he replied. "I just started toward you before I put on the robe, and you were ready to tear down a door getting away." His eyes searched hers. "You don't look much calmer right now, love," he added gently. "If you could have seen your face when I brought you in here . . ."

She swallowed. "You were so angry."

"What did you expect? I don't like having other men rammed down my throat," he said curtly. "Especially James Harris."

She half-smiled. "And I didn't like being told that I was an obligation."

He linked his hands behind her, flexing his powerful shoulders with the motion. "Which still doesn't answer me. I want you."

Her eyes dropped to the massive chest supporting her. She wanted him, too, but she wasn't blinded by passion, she was too aware of consequences, of motives. She was confused—utterly confused. How had this all happened between them?

He caught her chin and tilted her flickering eyes up to his. "I won't let you get pregnant. Is that what you're afraid of?"

The flush went from her hairline down to her throat in a slow, vivid flood, and he watched it with a dark scowl.

"What kind of men have you been with?" he asked with a rough chuckle. "Didn't you ever talk about sex, for God's sake?"

"Not a lot, no," she managed to blurt out.

"On the other hand," he murmured, easing

her down onto her back, "why talk about it at all?" His mouth brushed lazily across hers, a shimmer of exquisite sensation that he repeated again and again while his warm hands moved against her back, slipping her robe from her shoulders and then easing down the straps of her gown.

"Nick . . ." she whispered shakily under his warm, hard mouth as its expert pressure increased sensuously.

His hands eased up to her rib cage, his thumbs rubbing slowly, gently, at the sides of her breasts in a growing pattern that made her body rise toward him pleadingly.

"I've held back until I ache like an adolescent," he whispered against her throat. "My God, I've tried to give you enough time, but I'm running out of it." And this time, he meant business. There was no light, teasing pressure in it now. He kissed her with practiced skill, exploring every inch of her mouth with his lips, his tongue, his teeth.

His warm hands were on her breasts now, the gown somehow lowered to her waist, his fingers making incredible sensations flow through her taut body as they caressed her.

"Oh, Nick," she gasped, looking straight into his dark eyes as he lifted his head to look down at her.

His chest rose and fell heavily, and there was a faint dampness on the skin her fingers were pressed against. His eyes lowered to the high, bare curves of her breasts and he studied her as if he'd never seen a woman's body before, something thrilling in the bold intensity of his gaze.

"Nicholas," she whispered.

"What, love?" he asked softly.

Her hands reached up to touch his broad face, to trace the hard lines that never seemed to relax, even now. "I . . . I want to be . . . closer," she managed shakily.

His mouth gently crushed hers. "Do you?" he murmured. "How close, like this?" He eased his massive body over hers until it relaxed onto hers from breast to hip, his arms taking the bulk of his formidable weight.

"No," she whispered under his seeking mouth. "All . . . all of you, Nicholas," she murmured, gasping as she felt the crush of his body pressing her down into the mattress, making silvery waves of emotion surge through her slenderness. Her soft, bare breasts flattened under the rough, hard crush of his chest, and she could feel the pattern of the dark curling hair on it tickling as her arms reached up to hold him closer than she'd ever been to another living soul. She wanted desperately to please him, to give and give and go on giving until he burned with the same fires he was kindling in her.

"I want . . . to please you," she whispered into his rough, hungry mouth.

"You are pleasing me," he ground out. His mouth broke hers open, invading it intimately, hungrily. "God, your breasts are soft . . ."

She moved sensuously under him, feeling the crisp, dark hair on his massive chest make new and wild sensations run through her slender body.

"Am I too heavy?" he murmured against her eager mouth.

"No," she whispered achingly. Her eyes looked straight up into his as her tongue traced patterns along the chiseled line of his upper lip.

He watched her, his eyes dark and full of secrets, his chest throbbing against her breasts, his breath flaring through his nostrils.

"Do you always watch your women like this?" she asked unsteadily, pausing to run her fingers along the long, broad curve of his muscular back.

"Only when I've wanted them like hell for years," he replied. He pressed against her deliberately, making her feel the proof of his desire like a brand against her hips. "Do you feel how much?"

She caught her breath at the sensation, her legs going boneless, admitting the full weight of his body between them so that not one part of their bodies were separated.

He bent and kissed her again, thoroughly this time, the way he had that first day in the Rolls, with a thrusting, demanding pressure that made her body arch into his—that ripped a moan of pure pleasure from her throat.

She heard a soft, triumphant laugh and opened her eyes lazily, feeling a hundred tiny tremors raking her yielded body as his hands eased the rest of the gown away from her. The room was cool enough that she missed his warmth when he raised himself up to throw the gown over the side of the bed.

His dark eyes ate every inch of her, running up the long, smooth curve of her legs to the curve of her hips, the deep indentation at her waist, the thrust of her breasts. She had the strangest feeling that she would have minded that scrutiny from any other man. Even years back, James Harris had been too intent on possession to pay much attention to her young body. He'd been in a hurry and the result had been a blur of discomfort, embarrassment, and no pleasure at all for Keena.

But this was different. Nicholas was special to her in ways she'd never discovered until just lately. And to him she wasn't merely a body or a one-night stand. She was something quite different, she could see it in the dark, appreciative gaze he drew over her.

He bent and pressed his mouth to her soft, warm stomach, working his way up to her breasts, his hand smoothing her flesh, touching her in new ways, learning the sweet contours of her body while his lips and tongue and teeth fostered a riot of sensation that left her breasts tingling, her body hungry and writhing under the expert arousal.

Her fingers were tangled in his shaggy mane of hair, her eyes half wild as he rose to see the expression on her flushed face.

"You don't know how to give it back, do you?" he asked in a strange, husky tone, his powerful body pulsing with desire.

She touched his mouth with her fingers, fascinated by it, by the pleasure it gave. "Give what back?" she whispered. "I want you, Nick," she added softly. "You must know that by now."

"You aren't a virgin," he said, but it was a question.

She bit her lip. "No."

"Damn it, don't look like that," he ground

146

out, turning her averted face back to his. "I told you once that it didn't matter to me, and I meant it. But you don't act like an experienced woman. How careful am I going to have to be?"

She sighed weakly. "The first time . . . the only time . . . was with James," she admitted tightly. "It was uncomfortable, and hurried—" her voice broke off.

"Go on," he urged.

"I thought I'd die of shame when I found out that he hadn't any plans to marry me. He'd only wanted me, and he told his brother that it had been like . . . like making love to a man."

Nicholas didn't say anything. Not a word. He stared down at her with eyes she couldn't read in a face gone as hard as granite. Now he knew the agony that Harris had inflicted on her.

"Don't hate me . . ." she pleaded tearfully.

"Hate you, for God's sake!" he blurted out. He bent and crushed his mouth down on hers. "Does it feel as if I hate you, you little fool?"

Tears rolled down her cheeks. She clung to him, even as he sat up, drawing her across his lap to hold, to comfort. His big arms were warm and as pleasurable in a sense as they had been in passion. She nuzzled her face

147

against his throat, drinking in the scent of him, the feel of him.

"Nick?" she whispered.

"What, honey?"

She drew away and looked up at him. "Love me," she whispered.

He brushed a strand of hair away from the corner of her mouth, studying her lips with a hungry intensity, but he didn't make a move toward her.

"How do you feel about Harris now?" he asked, his dark eyes darting up to catch the surprise in hers.

"Now?" she echoed. "I . . . well, I don't know," she blurted out.

"Don't you think," he said gently, "that you'd better find out before you and I go any further?"

She searched his eyes, looking for answers that she couldn't find. It was like tracking a lion who didn't want to be found.

"Don't you want me?" she asked.

He took her hand and pressed it deliberately against his flat stomach, watching the color run into her face as she touched him.

One dark eyebrow went up and he smiled faintly. "I want you," he said. "But I'm not going to do a thing about it until you've put him back in the past where he belongs. You were a girl, Keena," he added seriously. "You thought he was sincere, and he wasn't. But there was no harm done. It's something that happened long ago." He lowered his dark head and brushed his mouth slowly, sensuously against hers, smiling against it when it parted and pleaded for something harder. "It doesn't have a damned thing to do with you and me."

She kissed him back in the same teasing, arousing manner. "Nick . . ." she pleaded.

He nipped her lower lip delicately. "Why did he say it was like making love to a man?" he murmured, deliberately making her face that specter. "Were you that thin?"

"Flat-chested," she corrected, her voice faintly bitter.

Nicholas drew back and looked down at her taut, firm breasts, his lips curving sensuously as he traced their soft curves. "You?" he chuckled.

"Oh, Nick," she breathed, her voice, her eyes, full of emotion as she reached up and clung to him, her cheek against his broad, strong chest, secure in the arms that held her, the hands that caressed her bare back.

"I hate to break this up," he murmured, "but even at my age, I can't sit with a gorgeous nude brunette in my lap for very long without doing something about it. Suppose you put your clothes on and I'll pour some coffee."

"I'd rather wrestle you down in the bed," she whispered. "If you'd just teach me how to seduce you . . ."

There was pure delight in his laughter, and more than that in the slow, warm embrace that followed it. "At my earliest opportunity," he promised.

She eased reluctantly out of his arms, off his lap, feeling strangely comfortable with him as she gathered up her gown and robe.

"Clothes," he said, dragging his sweater on as he went out the door, pausing to glance back at her with a musing smile. "You're far too tempting like that, even with a robe over you."

"You're very flattering, you know," she murmured from the safety of the robe while she searched for her slacks and blouse in the closet.

"No, love," he said quietly. "I meant every word."

He closed the door behind him, leaving her to dress.

Five minutes later she joined him on the sofa, wearing a black silk blouse over a pair of beige suede jeans, her hair in place, her face made up, her eyes full of Nicholas.

He whistled softly. "What an eyeful," he murmured approvingly. He handed her a cup of black coffee as she curled up near the arm of the couch before he leaned back with his own cup held in one huge hand.

"You told me once that you liked black-and-beige combinations best," she said without thinking.

"On you, yes." He sipped his coffee, watching her over the rim of his cup. "I can still taste you," he murmured, his eyes dark with passion, smiling when she averted her eyes. "Miss Sophistication," he chuckled. "I thought you were a woman of the world, even at the beginning. I was mad as hell at you about that crack you made the night I went to Paris." He lifted an eyebrow at her shocked expression. "I was out for revenge. I'd seen the way you looked at me in the elevator. I wondered how far I could get," he said, amusement in his tone. "It was a game. Nothing more than that. And then—"

The phone rang before he could finish, and Keena went to answer it with her pride around her knees. A game. A cruel game of which he should be ashamed as she was ashamed. To think that she let him look at her, touch her that intimately.

"Hello?" she asked numbly.

"Nicholas Coleman, please," came a cultured masculine voice from the other end of the line.

She held out the receiver without meeting his eyes. "For you," she said quietly.

She sat back down with her coffee, as wooden inside as the floor, feeling nothing at all. She vaguely heard Nicholas's deep, measured voice, now sharp, now questioning, for several minutes before he hung up the phone and turned back to her.

"Where was I?" he murmured darkly.

"Leaving," she replied, her eyes cold as they met his. "Good-bye."

"I wanted to explain something to you," he said quietly.

"I'm very busy. If I'm going to leave for Ashton in the morning, I've got a lot of work to do," she said tightly.

His eyes narrowed. "You're not going back alone," he warned.

"Why bother?" she asked haughtily. "The game's over, Nicholas. I'm not playing anymore."

"Neither am I, honey," he said softly, smiling faintly at her. "Not anymore."

She watched him go with a leaden feeling in her stomach.

"Thanks for breakfast," she managed politely.

He turned at the door, studying her slender, graceful body wistfully. "How would you like to see the plantation on the way to Ashton?"

The question stunned her. "Go to Charleston, you mean?"

He nodded. "We could spend a few hours there. I'd like to show it to you."

Would he really, or did he just want to visit his ghost and have her there to make it bearable for him? She wasn't sure of her footing with Nicholas anymore. She was more than a little frightened of him now.

"Keena, I won't try to take you to bed again," he said gently. "That's over."

She studied him for a moment before she nodded. "All right."

"I'll send Jimson for you at seven," he added, going out the door. "I want to get an early start."

"All right. I'll be ready."

A highly polished black Lincoln was waiting for them at the Charleston airport, with Jimson standing tall and dignified beside it.

"You think of everything," Keena murmured as they got into the spacious backseat.

"I have to, honey," he replied. "Jimson, go through town before we start home. I want to show Miss Whitman some of the city."

"Yes, sir," Jimson replied. "Where would you like to start, sir?"

"Turn down Meeting Street and down Broad," he replied, "then onto Church as far as St. Phillip's and the Pirate House. That's about all we'll have time for this trip."

"There are a number of interesting homes on East Bay and Tradd streets, sir," Jimson reminded him.

"Time, Jimson," he sighed, leaning back. "Time."

"Yes, sir," came the quiet reply.

Keena looked across the seat at him, her eyes hesitant, wary. But his eyes were closed, and there were deep new lines cut into his broad, hard face, and deep shadows under his eyes. She'd seen Nicholas in all sorts of conditions, but never this worn.

"Have you slept at all?" she asked softly.

"Not a lot, no," he replied. His eyes opened and looked straight into hers, searching them. "Did you, Keena?"

She looked away, her face rigid. "I never realized there were so many palm trees in this section of the state," she murmured, studying the old houses along the way as they began to get into city traffic. "How old is Charleston, anyway?"

"It was founded in 1670," Nicholas said, following her gaze to the fascinating examples of architecture—the Charleston double house, the Greek Revival style, the plantation house, and just about every other architectural style from a period of almost two centuries. "But the French Huguenots who settled here around fifteen years after that left the most lasting impression on the city. My ancestors, the St. Juliens, founded Manteau Gris."

"I'm sorry?" she murmured as the French flew right over her head.

"The plantation house. It means 'gray cloak,' but we cling to the old name," he replied. "The name comes from the Spanish moss—which is, by the way, neither Spanish nor moss— hanging from the huge live oaks along the river. The first house was built in 1769. It burned during the Revolutionary War, and all but the flooring and some of the timbers were destroyed. It was rebuilt, then it was burned again during the Civil War." He laughed softly. "Only a little of the original cedar remains. It was rebuilt that last time of Bermuda stone overlaid with stucco, and given a gray wash. It has heart pine flooring and some imposing woodwork, including a winding staircase that the staff keep polished to a glass sheen."

"You love it, don't you?" she asked, already seeing the rambling country house in her mind.

"Very much. The older I get, the more aware I am of my roots. Look," he said, sitting up to point out the window at her side. "That's St. Michael's Episcopal Church. It's the oldest church building in the city."

"How lovely," she murmured, her eyes on the tall spire as they passed the white structure.

"And down that way is what we call 'South of Broad.' It's the old section of the city. Restaurants serve our famous she-crab soup, made from the roe of the crab, along with roasted oysters and tiny Iceland lobsters in a special sauce. I'll have to take you there one day. There's too much to see to spend less than half a day browsing."

"I'd like that," she said quietly, drinking in the sights and sounds with a smile. "Nick, what about Fort Sumter," she asked, "and the Battery?"

"We'll go back that way," he assured her as Jimson made a right turn followed scant minutes later by a left turn. Two cross-streets later, Nicholas had Jimson slow down.

"The church is St. Phillip's Episcopal," he told her. "But this Bermuda stone house is known as Pirate House, and I used to haunt it when I was a boy." His dark eyes sparkled with merriment. "Rumor has it that pirates used to meet with respectable Charleston merchants here to barter."

"There were pirates in Charleston?" she exclaimed. "I thought they only sailed the West Indies."

"Stede Bonnet was one of the worst," he told her. "He was hanged in 1718 and his body was buried in the marshes near the Battery. There was a female pirate, too, a beautiful woman named Anne Bonney, the illegitimate daughter of an Irish merchant. She married a pirate named James Bonney, whom she later deserted in Nassau for another privateer named Calico Jack Rackham."

Keena, all big green eyes, prodded him. "And?"

"The ship was taken in Jamaica in 1720 and the crew brought to justice." He chuckled softly at the dismay in her face. "Maybe they got away," he murmured, and laughed again when she brightened.

"I'd love to go inside," she sighed as they passed the house.

"All apartments now," he replied. "But I

may be able to arrange something the next time we come here. "Back around by East Bay and the Battery, Jimson," he told the driver.

"Yes, sir."

Fort Sumter looked so peaceful sitting out in the harbor, and Keena eyed it wistfully as they passed it and drove along the Battery back into the city.

"It's hard to believe that wars were ever fought here," she told Nicholas.

"Charleston has had its share of problems over the years," he returned. "It was captured by the British in 1780, and fought valiantly during the Civil War. It's withstood hurricanes and an earthquake, but it's still standing. Stubborn, proud, and as eloquent as any southern statesman. I suppose that's why I have such a high regard for it."

"Do they have tours of these houses?" Keena asked.

He nodded. "Every spring. We're a few weeks too early."

Keena's first glimpse of Manteau Gris was enough to make her fall in love with it. The towering gray stone house sat far back off the road amid a nest of huge live oaks dripping with Spanish moss, along with magnolia trees, pine trees, and shrubs that must have been magnificent in bloom. There was a gray split-rail fence all the way around the grassy front lawn, with its circular driveway, and several small, attractive outbuildings, one of which was a gazebo.

"It's magnificent," Keena breathed reverently.

"That runs in the family," he murmured, catching her eye to remind her of the last, very embarrassing time she'd used that word.

"Who looks after it for you?" she asked.

"The housekeeper and her husband—the Collinses. They've been with the family since I was a teenager."

She studied his hard, unyielding face. "I can't imagine you as a teenager," she murmured.

"Can't you?"

"I'll bet you were born an adult," she replied with a faint smile.

"I had to be," he replied matter-of-factly. "My parents were never here. Mrs. Collins damned near raised me."

"Where were your parents?" she asked softly.

"In Cannes. Switzerland. Rome. Paris. Anywhere except here. They shared a common allergy—me."

She saw through that toughness and cynicism for just an instant to a lonely, wounded little boy, a dark-haired child who spent his free time sitting near the harbor watching the ships come and go and dreaming of pirates.

Her fingers reached out and very hesitantly touched the back of the broad, dark hand resting on the seat beside him.

He stiffened at the light contact and drew back, his eyes daring her to pity him as they cut across toward her.

She shifted, pretending an interest in the flat face of the house with its imposing woodwork and long front portico and steps, wide and cool looking, and she wondered how that coral would feel under hot, bare feet in the summertime.

"It's a house meant for children," she murmured without thinking.

He jerked open the door as Jimson lulled the engine to a full stop and got out, leaving Jimson to open the door for Keena. It was only then that she realized how much what she'd said must have hurt him.

She recalled belatedly that he and his first wife couldn't have children at all. She'd never bothered to ask why, whose problem it was. It had never occurred to her that it would have hurt a man like Nicholas, who was so very much a man, not to be able to have sons or daughters of his own.

Although she was still smarting from his treatment of her the day before, she'd never meant to deliberately hurt him. And if his stiff back was any measure of the wounding, it was going to take a truckload of finesse to make a balm. He looked more imposing, more unapproachable, than she'd ever seen him. And for the first time she wanted to get close to him in a more than physical way. She wanted to be a part of his life.

Seven

Keena stood very still and silent as that single thought penetrated. She wanted to be a part of his life. That had never happened before. She'd been studiously independent, needing no one, nothing but her own company, her career, to sustain her. But now she felt a deep, gnawing hunger for something more. For a man. For sharing, and quiet loving, and children.

But last night she'd already come to the conclusion, as she slept in that lonely room, that

Nicholas had only wanted her as a passing fancy. He'd said himself that he wasn't playing anymore. They were going to be friends again. Just friends. Because he'd never gotten over Misty and he had nothing more than desire to give a woman.

She followed him onto the front porch where a tall, buxom lady was giving him a hug, and an equally tall but thin old gentleman behind them smiled.

"Keena, this is Jesse Collins and his wife, Maude. They manage Manteau Gris for me," Nicholas said as she joined them, and there was a chorus of how do you dos before they went inside.

The wooden floors were spotlessly clean and waxed, and that spiral staircase Nicholas had mentioned was truly dazzling. As the huge double doors were closed, her eyes were drawn to the fanlight above them, and the slight imperfection of the glass in it hinted at its age.

A Persian rug graced the center hall, its pattern a mixture of burgundy, cream, and blue. There was a large front room just off to the left, its floors covered with other luxurious oriental rugs, its furniture mostly mahogany that glistened with polished brass fittings.

"The furniture," Keena asked softly, her

gaze moving from the gorgeous antiques to the paintings and then to the huge stone fireplace, "is it West Indian?"

"A discerning eye the young lady has," Mrs. Collins laughed, her whole broad face friendly and warm. "Yes, ma'am, it is. The first Mr. Coleman to own Grey Cloak," she glanced apologetically at Nicholas for using the English version, "married the daughter of a West Indian planter, and these pieces were part of her dowry. And I could tell you some tales about that pair, I could."

"But not before you bring us some coffee," Nicholas said with a smile. "It's been a long morning."

"And you working yourself to death into the bargain, I'll say," Mrs. Collins said disapprovingly. "What you need is a few weeks here, so that I can look after you proper. I'll fix some sandwiches and cake for you as well. You haven't had breakfast either, I don't imagine," she muttered as she left the room, closing the door behind her.

"They never let you grow up," he said quietly, shaking his head. His eyes roamed the room, as hers had. "I've missed this."

She studied his broad back in the dark brown suit, seeing the way the fabric strained across his powerful muscles. "I'm sorry about what I said. I didn't think."

He half-turned. "Will you stop apologizing?" he growled. "My God, that's all you do lately. You know you don't have to pull your punches with me. You never have."

She shifted her shoulders uncomfortably, helplessly. "But I didn't want you to think . . ."

His eyes darkened. "The problem was with Misty," he said shortly. "Not me. Even for my age I'm damned fertile. Tests don't lie."

"You had tests?" she asked softly.

"I had to," he murmured, turning, a hand restlessly combing through his dark hair, "for my own peace of mind. I had to know."

She didn't know what to say to him, how to find the words. A child would have been such a comfort to him in his grief. Of course, it had been six years, but did he still grieve? Did he still love Misty to the exclusion of everything else? Was that why he drove himself so relentlessly, even now?

He pulled a cigarette from his pocket and lit it. At least he'd cut down on that, she thought idly. He hardly smoked at all anymore.

She looked away. "I've sometimes wondered why you and Misty never had children, that's all."

"Well, now you know," he said simply. "It wasn't because I never wanted them, I did. I still do." He went to the window and stared out at the live oaks, bare of leaves, but still covered with the long curling strands of Spanish moss, dark gray against the gray winter sky.

She looked down at the floor. She had somehow managed to anger him again, to cause him to withdraw from her and she wished she'd never agreed to come here. It was more of an ordeal than she could have imagined. Just the sight of him hurt suddenly. Here they were, alone in the same room with only fifteen feet or so separating them. But she might as well have been in New York. Was this the pattern for their future? Had they lost even the friendship that they'd had?

She opened her mouth to tell him that she wanted to cut this visit short and go straight on to Ashton alone. But before she could get the words out, Mrs. Collins came bustling back in all smiles, with a heavily laden tray of snacks and coffee.

"Here we are," she cooed, setting the tray gently down on the coffee table. "Now you make the young lady eat something too, Mr. Nick," she admonished as she went out the door. "She needs some feeding up."

Keena kept her eyes lowered, reaching out to pour coffee into the cups. They were fine bone china, with a rose pattern, and very old.

"You should be properly flattered," Nicholas said, dropping into a huge armchair across from the sofa, holding the dainty cup and saucer easily in one hand. "Mrs. Collins rarely uses the rose china except for the most important visitors."

"I'm honored," she laughed bitterly. "I would think I hardly qualify."

"You do to some people—to Harris, surely?" he asked with a strange, cruel smile.

She shifted restlessly, sipping the blistering hot coffee. "Surely," she replied sarcastically.

"When are you planning this party to end all parties?" he asked carelessly.

Her eyes ricocheted off his and back to her cup. "Mandy sent out the invitations the day I left," she informed him. "She's already contacted the caterer and arranged for a band by now."

"How organized," he replied. He sipped his own coffee, reminiscent of some regal baron as he filled that massive chair.

"I am, after all, a businesswoman," she reminded him coolly.

"All business," he returned politely. "Very little woman."

She finished her coffee, refusing to let him see how he was hurting her. "How much longer are we going to be here?"

He leaned forward and put down his cup. "I thought you might like to see the grounds before we rush away," he said bitterly.

"If you can spare the time to show them to me," she returned with dripping sweetness.

They barely spoke as he led her out the back door and onto the yellowed grass. They walked under the tremendous gnarled branches of the oaks, and far away was the sound of the river running, the whisper of pines touching high above against the gray sky.

"The . . . the flowers must be lovely in bloom," she said.

"They are," he replied. "Azaleas, camellias, dogwood, magnolias, roses—it's a symphony of color in the spring and early summer."

"Your wife," she murmured, watching the leaves fly as her feet lifted them, "did she plant any of them?"

"Misty was too delicate for gardening," he said shortly. His eyes darted sideways to catch hers. "Why are you trying so hard to dredge up ghosts? Are you that afraid of me? I'm through trying to seduce you!"

"Yes, the game is over. Isn't that the way you

put it?" she broke out. To her horror, she felt the hot sting of tears filling her eyes.

His jaw clenched. "Oh, God, Keena," he ground out, moving toward her. He caught her arms and slammed her body against his, crushing her in a warm, hurting embrace. He rocked her against his warm, hard chest, and she could feel the heavy slam of his heart against her breasts, even through the layers of clothing that separated them. Her hands, flat against his shirtfront under the jacket, gloried in the warm strength of the concealed muscles.

"Can you imagine how I felt when I knew?" he whispered roughly, his voice muffled against her hair. "My God, I walked out of that apartment wanting to kill Harris." He drew in a deep, steadying breath, his arms contracting again. "Of course I didn't sleep, how could I? I'd wanted it to be perfect with us, absolutely perfect the first time we made love."

Tears flooded her face as she pressed her cheek to his broad chest. "I wanted you, you know," she managed tearfully.

"Yes," he said heavily.

She drew back and looked up at him with a watery smile. "It was delicious while it lasted," she choked.

"Was it?" he murmured, searching her eyes with a slight frown.

He traced her lips with one broad-tipped finger, watching it hungrily. "I don't dare imagine how much better it could have been," he whispered back. "You respond so wonderfully to me, my little love—so warm and giving and passionate. You very nearly drove me mad yesterday. And then not being able to have you after all . . ."

The memory of it made her heart go wild. Her body trembled with it, her eyes told him how it had been for her.

"I want you," she whispered shakily.

"I want you too," he replied quietly. "But for the time being, we're going to let it stand the way it is between us."

She hit his broad chest in silent frustration. "Nicholas!"

"Do you honestly think you're ready for that kind of commitment?" he asked harshly.

Her green eyes were wide and confused as they looked up into his.

His hands held her in front of him, firmly caressing her upper arms through the soft oyster-white jacket of her suit. "Keena, sex is a responsibility," he said gently. "Unless it's understood as a business proposition, there's more to it than the easing of an ache. Have

171

you thought about precautions?" he asked levelly.

She felt very young when he asked questions like that. "Not really," she replied.

He smiled. "Well?"

She glanced at him and down again. "You take care of it."

He laughed softly. His eyes were patient, gleaming with quiet amusement. "With you? Like hell I could. When I managed to tear myself away from you yesterday, I didn't know my name. No, honey, don't expect me to take care of it. I thought I could at the beginning, but I'm wiser now."

She traced the button on his shirt. "Aren't men supposed to be more in control of themselves at your age, Mr. Coleman?" she teased gently.

His fingers trailed down her throat to trace the high, full thrust of her breasts. "Not when they want a woman the way I want you," he murmured. "Why do you bother with a bra?"

She could hardly breathe for the slam of her heart as those slow, very wise fingers did impossible things to her self-control.

Her hands slid up to his broad, strong neck and her nails tangled in the thick hair at its nape, her eyes closed while he touched and teased.

"Look at me," he whispered huskily.

She raised her misty eyes to his, watching the darkness grow in them as he undid, one by one, the buttons on her blouse. Her lips parted under a rush of breath, but she didn't make an effort to stop him.

His hands started to reach around her for the clasp of her bra, but she shook her head slowly, her eyes never leaving his.

"It fastens . . . in front," she whispered shakily.

"Do you want to be touched?" he asked as he found the catch and very slowly loosened it, his fingers brushing the wispy lace away from the high, perfect curves of her breasts.

"Only by you," she managed in a tight, muffled voice.

His hands swallowed her, took the soft weight of her, caressed and cherished and warmed her while she bit hard on her lower lip to keep from crying out, her eyes involuntarily closing.

"Sweet, sweet love," he whispered, lowering his dark head. "Kiss me."

She reached up and drew his mouth down onto hers, letting her lips part, inviting him, luring him, her body trembling as if with a fever as his mouth bit into hers with a hunger that was incredibly tender, loving, deeper than anything they'd ever shared. They rocked together, a tremor shaking his body as hers quaked with the kiss that locked them together for all of one long, breathless, aching minute.

He drew back a breath, his eyes dropping to the soft white treasure swallowed in his big hands, and he bent suddenly to put his mouth reverently to each hard pink tip, the moistness making the cold seem unusually fierce to Keena as it brushed her bareness.

"We must both be out of our minds," he whispered as he refastened the catch and buttoned the blouse back into place. "You'll have pneumonia."

"It's so beautiful when you touch me," she told him with a piercing tenderness in her soft eyes, "when you look at me. Nicholas, I'll never let another man touch me like that."

"I know," he said tightly. "Keena, you're the most beautiful thing I've ever seen. I could eat you from head to toe, do you know that? Every soft, pearly inch of you, God!" He ground her body against his, holding her so close she could barely breathe. "I could take you here on the ground," he breathed harshly. "Oh, God, I hurt!"

"I'm sorry," she whispered, soothing him, her hands comforting, warm, and tender as she smoothed his hair and crooned. "I know, I know. Nicholas, you can have me," she whispered into his ear. "Right now, right here, standing up, lying down, any way at all, don't you know that?"

"Yes, I know," he whispered tautly, but with some measure of control. His big arms tightened. "You've always been willing to give me anything I needed. Even sex, is that how it goes?"

"I'd do anything for you," she said simply, meeting his eyes as he lifted his leonine head. "Anything in the world."

"Why?" he asked quietly, and searched her eyes deeply while he waited for her to answer him.

She blinked, vaguely confused by the question. "Because . . . I care about you," she said finally. "Because we're friends."

"Would you really give yourself to me out of friendship alone?" he asked very gently.

"You're confusing me!"

"I think we're confusing each other," he replied dryly. He bent and brushed his mouth gently across hers. He laughed softly. "Can you imagine what making love on the ground would have done to that suit you're wearing?" he teased.

She flushed, but she didn't look away. "Shades of Hemingway," she murmured.

"We don't have a sleeping bag," he pointed out.

"The earth moved, anyway," she laughed, lowering her hot face.

"It did for me, too, honey," he murmured against her forehead. He linked his hands behind her and drew back, his chest lifting with a deep sigh. "Have your damned party, if it means so much to you. But you can't have Harris. Not now."

Wanting to irritate him, just for mischief, she grinned up at him and asked, "Why not?"

But he wasn't playing. "Because you're mine," he said quietly.

She studied him curiously. "I don't understand."

"Remind me to explain it to you when you've got this crazy scheme out of your system." He jerked her playfully. "What the hell does it matter now what happened nine years ago, Keena?" he wanted to know. "It's in the past, where it's best left, including the man you thought you couldn't live without. What kind of life could you have with him?"

"Nick . . ." she protested weakly.

"We have to live in the present. But I can see I'm going to have to let you find that out for yourself." He let her go and moved away to light a cigarette.

She stared after him until he noticed that he was walking alone and turned to wait for her.

"I don't understand," she said blankly.

"What?" he asked.

"You . . . you want me, but you won't do anything about it, and we're friends, but we're not," she stammered. "Nick, what do you want with me? What do you want from me?"

His dark eyes ate her from her jet black hair to her black and white pumps. "Honey, you'd be amazed."

"I already am," she murmured. "You could have any woman you wanted . . ."

"You're the only one who's never wanted me," he returned, "or my money."

"Is that why?" she persisted.

He turned away. "We'll have to talk about it someday. But not now, honey, I've got work to do. We'd better hit the road."

In no time at all, it seemed, they were back at the rambling old house in Ashton. Mandy smothered her with kisses and rattled off about the invitations, the decorator's bill, the caterers, the lack of phone calls, and half a dozen related subjects until Nicholas's rigid posture in the hall caught her eye and she vanished with a quick smile into the kitchen.

"Don't you want coffee?" Keena asked him.

He shook his head. His big hands were deep in his pockets and he looked strangely alone, standing by the door, his eyes quiet and faintly sad.

"You didn't bring your valises in," she added.

"I've already had them sent back to New York," he replied. A faint smile touched his hard mouth. "I'm not staying."

She should have been relieved. She should have shouted for joy and jumped up and down. But instead she felt a foreign urge to bawl and scream.

"Why not?" she asked.

"Business, love," he replied. "Things I can't handle from here. A labor dispute in the knitting mill, an equipment breakdown in Chattanooga . . . and on it goes."

"But you said—"

"I know what I said," he agreed. "Keena, you're a grown woman. I can't protect you from life, no matter how much I might want to. There's something called trust in any worthwhile relationship. It's time I let go of you, love. It's time I let you stand alone."

Her heart felt like heavy stone in her chest.

"But, Nick, you'll miss the party," she said plaintively.

One corner of his mouth went up. "Send me an invitation."

She returned the smile a little shakily. "I'll do that. Nick, you aren't still angry at me?" she asked with a burst of apprehension. "You aren't saying good-bye . . ."

He went toward her, catching her waist with two big, warm hands to draw her unresistingly against his body, so that she could feel every inch of him touching her.

"Good-bye isn't a word we're ever going to use," he said gently. "I'm giving you some breathing room, that's all. We've come a long way in a little time, but you've got to be sure. I've said that before, now I'm saying it again. Have your party. Get Harris out of your system. Spend some time with him. But, nothing further, Miss Liberty," he warned, something dangerous in his gaze. "Not unless you tell me first. I want your word on that."

She had to force herself to speak. "You sound very possessive," she whispered.

"You belong to me," he replied simply. "I'm not handing you over to any other man unless I'm damned sure it's right for you, and that's why I want a promise. Now."

"All right," she agreed without knowing why she did it.

He nodded. "And if you need me, you know where I am."

Her hands smoothed his shirtfront, already feeling the pain of separation. "Will you call me?"

"No."

"Why not?" she asked, incredulous.

"I'll be busy. Remember that invitation."

"Yes, Nicholas." It was going to be worse than ever. Even when he left the country, he called her. She felt desolation move over her like an icy wind.

"What a sad little voice," he murmured gently. "None of that. Smile for me."

She raised her sad eyes to his. "I don't feel like smiling. I'll miss you."

He searched her face. "I hope so," he murmured. "So long, my own."

She studied his mouth. "Are you going to kiss me?" she whispered.

"If you want me to."

She glowered at him and moved away. "Never mind, if it's such a trial to you."

He laughed softly, and she waited for his hard arms to come around her, her eyes closed, a dreaming smile on her mouth. A minute later she heard the door open.

She whirled, shock in her eyes, but he didn't look back. He closed the door behind him.

"Nick," she whispered in anguish.

She ran after him, but he was already down the steps, and by the time she got to the top step, he was cranking the Rolls's soft engine.

She folded her arms tight over her breasts, hurting. She didn't understand Nicholas or herself, but she understood the ache within. She felt alone, as she hadn't felt since her early teens. She felt completely, hopelessly, alone and she didn't know how she was going to go on living without Nicholas somewhere in her life. Had he said good-bye forever, and all that talk about coming to the party and giving her some freedom was nothing but a placebo? Oh, Nicholas!

Eight

In six years it was the first time she'd gone more than two weeks without seeing or hearing from Nicholas. As the days passed, she felt herself withering, a flower without sunlight to sustain it.

James, whose company had entertained her once or twice a week, barely seemed to notice that she wasn't overly communicative. He enjoyed talking more than listening, anyway, and he didn't know Keena well enough to sense that there was anything wrong.

At her encouragement he'd contacted Nicholas, and the mill was in the process of being gobbled up by Coleman Textiles. But not one word about Keena had entered the negotiations. She had probed carefully in an effort to find out, and had been disappointed at the answer. After all those years of friendship, had Nicholas really forgotten about her? Didn't he care?

"You're seeing a lot of that Harris man," Mandy commented one night as Keena waited for James to pick her up.

Keena only shrugged, tugging the cowl neckline of the pale green silk that washed down her slender body like a second skin. It was a simple design, but elegant enough even for Ashton's best restaurant.

"Nick doesn't care," she said bitterly. "He hasn't bothered to call, and it's been three weeks! The party is Friday night," she added, which was only two days away.

"He got an invitation," Mandy murmured. "I sent it by itself to make sure."

Keena's full mouth pouted. "He won't come."

"I wouldn't count on that." She admired the dress and smiled. "Very pretty. Does Mr. Harris appreciate the effort?"

She laughed softly. "He appreciates my encouraging him to ask Nicholas about buying the plant, that's all. He's a nice man, Mandy. A little devious, a little boyish, but very nice."

"Only that?" Mandy asked.

Keena sighed. "Yes. Isn't it sad? All these years I couldn't wait to come back and have my revenge on James for all that humiliation I thought I suffered from him and his friends. And do you know what? Nicholas was right. What attracted me the most about James was that I couldn't get him nine years ago. How sad."

"And, Nicholas?" Mandy asked softly.

Keena's fingers pleated the soft jersey nervously. "He doesn't care about me," she repeated.

"You can't cage a wild sparrow," Mandy said, in one of her enigmatic moods. "You have to free it and hope it will fly back to you."

Keena stared at her. "Have you been into the brandy?"

The doorbell sounded and Keena paused just long enough to grab up her red fox jacket and toss it over her shoulders. Nicholas would love the new addition to her wardrobe, she thought bitterly. It would only reinforce his pet name for her. She wrapped it close, and in her mind she felt again the hard crush of his bare arms, the feel of his body against hers, bare and hard and all masculine perfection. And she wanted him even more now than she had then. Wanted him in every way there was.

"You're very quiet," James said later as they finished the creamy dessert they'd been served with second cups of rich black coffee and cream.

Keena smiled apologetically. "I'm tired. Making preparations, you know."

"Oh, yes." He leaned back in his chair, the picture of elegance, smiling. "Everyone's talking about it. Imagine, a famous fashion designer in our midst, and all those sophisticated New Yorkers," he grinned. "I hear you've even invited some Broadway stars."

"You're right," she laughed. "Betty Sims and Jack Jackson," she added, naming two top performers from one of the newest hit shows, who were good customers as well as good friends. "Not to mention Demp Cashley."

"Cashley? The star pitcher for the—"

"Himself," she replied. "It's going to be quite a bash."

"And cost you quite a bundle," he added, and she could see the dollar signs adding up in his eyes.

She leaned back, shrugging lightly. "I can afford it," she murmured.

"So I hear. And see," he added, noting the

emerald bracelet that she'd redeemed by paying off the loan. He grimaced. "What a skyrocketing success. From poverty to the top of the heap in nine short years."

"With a little work in between," she reminded him.

He shook his head. "And none of us thought you had it in you," he sighed. "Me, most of all. When I think about some of the callous things I used to say about you . . ."

"I remember," she said, and the cut was less sharp than usual. "You said that I didn't belong in the same company with you and your friends, and that your mother would be horrified to find me there. I was standing around the corner from you when you said it."

He looked faintly shocked. "You didn't hear the rest?" he asked softly.

She stared at him. "What rest?"

"That I thought my mother was a horrible snob and if she opened her mouth to you, I'd give her hell," he replied quietly.

She couldn't believe her ears. "But you also said that awful thing about making love to me . . ."

"I was furious at Larry because of the way he was looking at you." he replied coolly. "I'd wanted to ask you to the party myself, but I wasn't sure you'd go because I was so much older." He smiled. "Earlier, you'd been so sweet to tease and take around places, until that night we were in Jack's apartment. Then I began to get serious.

"It would never have worked, you know. My mother would have destroyed you, and I hadn't reached the point of being independent financially. It was hopeless, and I saw it. So I broke it off. That party simply precipitated things. You left town before I was able to explain it to you." He looked sheepish. "I was frankly glad about that. I'd dreaded it."

"And I never dreamed the truth," she murmured, searching his blue eyes.

"It's just as well," he said quietly. "We're older now, more mature. This time we could make a go of it, and there's no one to interfere."

That's what you think, she told herself mentally, but she only smiled at him. She couldn't tell him that the man he was today could hardly take the place of the much younger man she'd loved as a teenager. Been infatuated with, she corrected herself. Love lasted, and this hadn't. Nicholas had been right all along. Nicholas . . .

"What would you say," he murmured, "to a nice, old-fashioned engagement ring?"

She mulled over her answer before she gave

it. "I'm very fond of you," she began. "I've enjoyed going out with you again, and I'm grateful to you for telling me the truth. But we're different people now. I've changed too much, James, to be satisfied by what you have to offer. I'm not eighteen anymore, you see," she ended sadly. "I grew up."

He flexed his shoulders with a wistful little smile. "I wish I hadn't," he murmured. "You were such a lovely little girl. If only . . ."

"Sad words, my friend," she said, reaching impulsively across the table to touch his hand. She smiled into his blue eyes. "I do like you very much."

He smiled back. "You're not bad yourself. How about another cup of coffee?"

She nodded. He had made it so easy for her. She smiled with relief.

"You have a lovely smile," he said simply, smiling back. "You always did." He motioned to the waiter. "Here, I'll get us a refill."

The night of the party finally came. Keena had designed something unique for it—a royal blue dress in deep, iridescent satin with gold swirls at the strapless bodice, the nipped waist, and the hem of the full skirt. It had a stole of matching fabric, and the design was worth a small fortune. In it, Keena looked absolutely queenly.

But her mind wasn't on her looks or her dress. It was on whether or not Nicholas was going to be among her illustrious guests. Her heart pounded at just the thought of seeing him again, of being held in his arms even in an insignificant dance. She'd missed him as she'd never dreamed it was possible to miss another human being, and if he didn't come, she didn't know how she was going to bear the evening.

She made her entrance after half the guests had already arrived. The rambling house was filled with sounds of laughter and music. High society mingled with local culture; Broadway stars chatted with the president of the local utility company. And everyone seemed to be having a wonderful time.

James was standing at the foot of the staircase when she came down, all eyes and approving smiles. But Keena's eyes were already darting around, looking for a dark head towering over everyone, for an imposing-looking man in evening clothes. But she didn't find it. Nicholas wasn't there.

"Don't look so somber," James teased. "You're gorgeous, and just take a peek at the stares you're drawing."

She didn't tell him that she couldn't have cared less, even though one pair of approving, kind eyes belonged to one of her worst female enemies in high school. All of a sudden the past didn't matter. Only one thing did—and that was Nicholas.

She liked the band Mandy had found. There were six of them, and they played some of the prettiest music Keena had heard short of New York. She found herself paying more attention to them than she did to her dancing partners, most of whom wanted to rave about her success.

James rescued her from one particularly heavy-footed partner who managed to squash one of her toes before she got away from him.

"Thanks," she murmured weakly. "My feet were in danger of being permanently damaged."

"My pleasure." He studied her wan little face. "Keena, you're very depressed tonight. Can I help?"

Only by becoming considerably taller, brawnier, and developing brown hair and eyes, she thought, but she only smiled and shook her head.

"I'm just tired," she lied. "I've had a lot of coordinating to do between here and my office. But the mad rush is temporarily over, and things will get better."

Of course they would. After all, the party had been in full swing for more than two hours, and there was still no sign of Nicholas.

She grabbed a Scotch and water from a passing waiter's tray and finished it in three large gulps. It had been a long time since she'd had hard liquor, but she didn't think about that. In fact, she grabbed a whiskey sour to top it off with, and only moments later she felt suddenly brighter.

She melted into James's arms, to his delight, and didn't make a sound when he bent and brushed his mouth across her cheek and in her hair when his arms caught her scandalously close as they danced.

And as fate would have it, that was the moment Nicholas Coleman chose to enter the room, resplendent in black evening clothes with a stark white shirt, bow tie, and a scowl black enough to curdle milk.

Nine

She stared at him across James's thin chest, her eyes as wide and uncomprehending as if she'd seen three ghosts playing jump rope.

He looked back, and his eyes weren't throwing roses at her.

She pried herself away from James with a nervous laugh as the big man came straight toward them.

"Mr. Coleman," James said politely, offering his hand and a smile.

Nicholas ignored both. He had eyes only for Keena. "I'd like to talk to you," he said shortly.

"Yes . . . of course," she stammered. "James, if you'll excuse me . . ."

"Of course," James replied courteously, moving away to get himself a drink.

"Hello, Nicholas," she said. Her eyes had trouble focusing on him, but he looked as big and dark and imposing as ever, and she noticed traces of his fiery French ancestry not for the first time in that flinty expression.

"Did you invite everyone south of Charleston?" he asked, casting a quick eye around the room.

"Only the very *best* people," she said haughtily and with a mischievous smile. She held out her arms. "Dance with me," she pouted.

"I'd rather take poison," he said shortly.

Her face fell tragically. All the weeks of waiting, of standing by windows looking out, hoping to see that ridiculous white car—weeks of jumping every time the phone rang, hoping it would be him. For this.

She turned and went ahead of him out of the big front room that had been cleared for dancing, across the hall to the small study. She waited for him to join her before she closed the sliding doors and sat down in the nearest chair.

"Sorry I can't offer you a drink," she said tautly, "unless you'd care to brave the crowd again."

He was smoking, his fingers lifting the cigarette to his mouth with jerky precision.

"Enjoying yourself?" he asked with a sharp glare.

"Up until about five minutes ago, yes, thanks," she replied with equal venom.

He walked to the darkened window and stood staring blankly out of it, smoking quietly while the strains of a familiar love song echoed through the house, through the tense silence that stretched between them.

"Realizing your dreams, little fox?" he asked with his back to her.

"Right now it feels more like a nightmare," she murmured, dropping her hands to her full, stiff skirt. It misted under her gaze. "I missed you," she whispered miserably.

"It looked like it," he agreed, his voice smooth with sarcasm.

She couldn't bear that hard, level gaze. "I had a Scotch and water, followed by a whiskey sour, and I'm feeling it, all right?"

"Why were you drinking?"

She clammed up. Not for worlds would she admit to this cold stranger that she'd wanted him beyond bearing, and the liquor had been nothing more than a painkiller.

"I just came to tell you that I'm transferring some of my smaller cuts to Harris's plant," he said quietly, his back still to her so that she missed the expression on his face. "Yours is going to be one of them. You'll deal directly with him."

"But . . . he sold you the plant," she murmured.

"He still has the management of it," he replied coolly. "Didn't he mention it?"

She shook her head. Her world was falling apart. Was he telling her to get out of his life?

"Are . . . are we going to see each other anymore, Nicholas?" she asked hesitantly.

He took a long draw from the cigarette before he answered her. "It might be wiser if we didn't, Keena."

She'd never taken a killing blow, but this felt like one. She hurt in a way she'd never imagined, as if he'd torn out her heart. She could hardly bear the pain.

Her eyes memorized him, every line of that huge, wrestler's frame, his shaggy, dark hair, the leonine features of his face, the nose she'd traced, the chest her fingers had explored so thoroughly, the square jaw that—set as it was now—spoke volumes on immovability. He was telling her good-bye for good, and there wasn't a thing she could say or do to make him change his mind.

She'd been right from the first. He'd wanted her, but only for a brief affair, and now he was easing her out of his life. It was what she knew he was planning, but even then she'd hoped against hope that she was wrong.

She stood up, very regal in her royal blue satin, too proud to let him see the anguish in her eyes.

"If that's what you think best," she said gently. "Thank you for . . . for everything, Nicholas. We've had some good times together."

He nodded. "They outnumbered the bad."

She met his eyes and turned quickly away before he could see the tears. "You might remember to send me a Christmas card next year," she said, fighting to control her voice, to keep it light.

"I'll do that."

She stopped in the hallway, still with her back to him. "Have a safe trip home, won't you?" she managed.

"You might at least turn around and look at me when you're saying good-bye," he growled harshly.

"No, I don't think I can do that," she whispered as the first of the tears rolled down her cheeks. She all but ran to James, hiding her tearful face against his spotless black jacket. Above the sound of the band, she winced when she heard the door open and close firmly.

"So that's how it is," James murmured gently.

But she couldn't answer him. She felt raw and wounded inside.

She managed somehow to survive the rest of the evening, smiling at her guests, saying all the right things, taking compliments with finesse, handing them out sometimes with sheer grit. She carried it off perfectly, and it wasn't until every single guest had gone home that she collapsed in tears on the sofa.

Mandy smoothed her tousled hair, cooed comforting words, pried that last confrontation with Nicholas out of her, and finally dried the tears.

"Did you tell him you weren't interested in James?" Mandy asked gently.

"No," came the sharp reply.

"Don't you realize what it must have looked like when he walked in and saw you dancing like that with him?"

She shifted restlessly. "I couldn't tell him, not after he'd literally moved me out of his life. I have to deal with James now." She wiped the tears from her cheeks. "At least it will give me a reason not to go back to New York for a while. I think I'll move my office down here, too, and Ann and Faye . . ."

"You like it here, dear, but they may not," Mandy reminded her.

"Then I'll commute." Her face clouded up again. "I don't want to see Nicholas again, ever," she wept, and her slender body collapsed again on the sofa. "I can't! I can't bear it, Mandy, I can't!"

"Do you hate him so much, sweetheart?" Mandy asked her.

"I love him," Keena corrected, lifting a tear-wet face to her housekeeper's kind eyes. "I didn't even discover it until we got to Charleston, and it was already too late. Mandy, I do love him so, and all I have in the world won't amount to one single day with him, do you know that? All the money and fame in the world isn't worth anything without Nicholas."

"May I make a suggestion?" Mandy asked.

"Is it reasonable?"

"Why don't you go and tell him how you feel?"

"And have him pat me on the back and soothe me?" Keena asked on a sob. "Because that's what he'd do. I'm just another responsibility to him. One he's grown tired of."

"Has it ever occurred to you that Nicholas might be in love with you?" Mandy asked in a soft, gentle tone.

"You didn't hear him," came the wailing reply.

"Amazing," Mandy sighed, "how he came two thousand miles in the middle of the night to see someone he hates."

Keena blinked. "He . . . he only came to tell me about the changeover."

"He could have done that on the phone. And what, pray tell, was the first thing he saw when he walked in the door?"

She shrugged. "Me. And James."

"Nick's always been wildly jealous of you," Mandy reminded her. "You may not have noticed it as much as I did. I've seen him watching you, honey, and most women would give anything to be looked at like that by a man like Nick. You think about it."

Keena's lower lip trembled, her eyes watered. "But what can I do? It's too late."

"Oh, no, it's not. You just wait right there." Mandy got up and left the room, and a minute later Keena heard her dialing. Three phone calls later she was back.

"I've got a plane waiting at the airport to

take you to Charleston, and a driver waiting there to take you to Nicholas's house. The rest is up to you," she said.

"I—I'll have to change." she murmured, looking down at the satin dress.

"Why bother?" Mandy asked. "You'll just be wasting time. Get a move on, honey, he's only there for the night!"

"Well, what about a cab?"

"There it comes," Mandy murmured with a grin. She kissed the younger woman. "Give Nick my love."

Without stopping to think, Keena wrapped the stole around her and ran out the door.

The manor house was quiet when she got out of the cab in front of it, but she girded up her courage and knocked on the door. The worst thing that could happen would be that Nicholas would throw her out. At any rate, she had to try. She loved him, and her pride wasn't going to sustain her through the long, empty years without him. She might as well risk everything.

Mrs. Collins ambled to the door in a long dressing gown, her face alternately astonished and delighted when she saw Keena standing at the door.

"Saints alive!" she exclaimed. "Now talk

about coincidences, Miss Keena. Remind me to tell you one day about how the first Mr. Coleman found his wife-to-be on his doorstep late one night. Did you come to see Mr. Nick?" she added, her voice stealthy.

Keena only nodded. Her heart jumped. "He . . . he is here?"

"Oh, he's here," Mrs. Collins sighed. "Roaring around upstairs for the better part of two hours, he was, throwing things about. He came here in a devil of a mood." Her old eyes twinkled. "I'm hoping you'll improve it, ma'am."

"I'll do my best," Keena promised.

But all her bravado threatened to leave her when she was climbing the long, dark staircase up to Nicholas's room. It was now or never. But suppose Mandy had read the whole situation wrong? Suppose Nicholas meant every word he said? He wouldn't appreciate being chased. He wasn't the kind of man who would.

She paused just outside his door. There was a sliver of yellow light peeking out from under it. Obviously he wasn't asleep, although no sound came from the other side of the heavy door.

Well, it was why she'd come, wasn't it, to talk to him? She couldn't do it from the hall.

She took a deep, sharp breath and opened the door.

She walked in before she had time for second thoughts, and closed it behind her. It was just as well that she had something to lean against, because Nicholas was stretched out on the bed without a stitch of clothing on, his dark eyes incredulous as they met hers.

"This," he said with faint humor, "is getting to be a habit with you."

She swallowed down a surge of embarrassment, her eyes involuntarily touching every powerful line of him. "Is it my fault that you won't wear pajamas?" she asked, trying to be nonchalant about it.

He laughed shortly. "May I ask what brings you here in the middle of the night?" he asked. "Isn't Harris enough for you?"

She girded her pride around her, only to let it fall again when she met those dark, devastating eyes. "I don't want James," she said quietly.

He cocked a dark eyebrow at her. "No? That wasn't what it looked like earlier."

Her lower lip trembled. "What did you expect, damn you?" she burst out. "You stayed away for almost a month, without calling or coming to see me. I spent all that time looking out windows, listening for the phone. Then, the night of the party, I jumped every time the doorbell rang, waiting, hoping . . . and you didn't come!" Tears misted her eyes. "I wanted you so, and you . . . didn't come. So I—I had a few drinks," she laughed tearfully, "and I danced with James. And I . . . hated you with all my heart."

He hadn't said a word, moved a muscle. But now he threw his powerful legs over the side of the bed and stood up.

"Are . . . aren't you going to put on a robe?" she asked, her voice wildly high-pitched as he approached her.

"Why bother?" he asked. "I'd just have to take it off again."

"B-but . . ." she stammered as he stopped just in front of her, his big, bare, muscular arms trapping her against the door, his hair-rough chest making a fleshy wall in front of her.

"Don't stop now, honey," he murmured, watching her expression. "It was just getting interesting. Why did you want me at the party?"

She stared straight ahead at the hard muscles of his massive chest. "Does it matter?" she asked tightly. "You think I'm sleeping with James, don't you?"

He moved closer so that she had to look up

or have her nose crushed against him. "You wouldn't have come this far, this fast, if you were," he murmured, letting his eyes lower to her soft mouth. "You'll go through that door if you try to get any closer to it," he whispered sensuously. "Why don't you stop fighting and do what you really want to do, Keena?"

She studied his broad, hard face. "What do I want to do?" she whispered shakily.

For an answer he caught her cold, nervous hands and placed them on his lean, warm hips, moving them up and across until they followed the arrowing of dark hair up his body to tangle them in the crisp, soft hair on his chest.

"This," he murmured as he bent to brush his mouth slowly, gently, against hers. "You want to touch me all over. You want to lie in my arms and feel my body over yours, taking absolute possession of it. Or are you going to tell me that's not why you came?"

Tears welled in her eyes. He was right. Of course he was. But it was more than that, so much more. She relaxed in his close embrace, letting his mouth have hers, letting his tongue reach into the dark, sweet warmth of her mouth to taste it, to probe and tease and kindle fires that flamed through her slender body like an explosion of sensation.

She moaned achingly, feeling every muscle in her body contract before she arched it uncontrollably against the massive warmth of his, feeling it fit exactly into the hard contours of his powerful body until even the air couldn't have managed to pass between them.

His hands caught the backs of her thighs and pressed her hips roughly into his, pressing her against him in a slow, sweet rotation that made her murmur against his mouth.

"Tell me it won't . . . be just . . . sex," she pleaded against his devouring mouth.

"It wouldn't have been just sex if I'd taken you six years ago," he ground out, drawing back just enough to let his fierce gaze capture her startled eyes. "My God, you've tied me up like a sheaf of grain, didn't you know? I meant it to be a game before I went to Paris, I needed to feel whole again when Maria and I broke up. But, my God, honey, you haunted me the whole time I was gone. When I came back, when I kissed you for the first time, the whole thing blew up in my face." He slid his hands up to her hips, pressing them sharply against his. "I wanted you this much the day we met, but the time was never right. Maybe that was a good thing, because I want a hell of a lot more from you now than this sexy young body."

"What . . . what do you want, Nicholas?"

she whispered at his lips, while her hands began, tentatively, to explore his bronzed torso.

He looked straight down into her eyes, his own beginning to flare up with dark lights. "I want you to give me a child."

She felt the words as if they'd touched her physically. "Why?" She mouthed it more than said it.

He laughed shortly. "Because I'm insanely in love with you, you crazy little witch," he growled softly, bending to lift her completely off the floor in his hard arms, crushing his mouth down against hers in a kiss that was as passionate as it was possessive. "Oh, God, I love you," he whispered into her mouth, "need you, want you. Keena, I wanted to kill Harris for just holding you, for touching you. I won't ask more than you can give me, but let me have you tonight. Stay with me."

Tears burned in her eyes as she returned the soft, clinging kisses, her eyes slitted, her breath coming in shuddering gasps.

"It . . . it may take more than one night," she managed shakily.

"What?" he murmured as he laid her down in the crisp brown sheets that still bore traces of the heat from his big body.

"For . . . to get . . ."

"For a child?" he whispered, his eyes more

tender than she'd ever seen them, his hands gentle as he smoothed the folds of the dress from her body to leave her clad only in her brief panties beneath his slow, possessive gaze. "In that case, it might be a good idea if you married me," he murmured. "To keep the gossip down, of course."

Her hands reached up to his neck and drew him down to her. "As if you cared about gossip, you blackguard," she whispered, glorying in the feel of his hands sliding over her, the newness of his eyes eating every soft, pink inch of her. It was magic, like a fantasy coming true, and tears welled up in her eyes at the intensity of love she felt. "Oh, Nick, I'd do anything you wanted me to," she whispered fervently. "Anything. I'd be your mistress, if that was all I could have. I'd give you a child and disgrace myself forever and not even count the cost."

His dark eyes stared into hers for a long, sweet moment. "You said something similar out on the grounds, not so very long ago. I asked you why you'd do anything for me, and you said you didn't know. Don't you, really?"

Her fingers touched his hard, warm mouth. "It's because I love you, my darling," she whispered tearfully. "Because you're the beginning and end of my whole world."

His eyes closed briefly, and when they opened again, there was a look in them that shattered her. "God knows, you're that and more to me, love. And one more thing. I loved my first wife. But not in the same way that I love you. I'm not living with ghosts, and there won't be any between us, not tonight or any other night."

"When did you know," she whispered, "that you loved me?"

He smiled tenderly. "I knew for sure when I drove up in your front yard and saw you flirting with Harris. I wanted to set fire to his trousers." His hands moved to take slow, sweet possession of her slender body. "But we'll talk about the whens and wherefores later. Right now, Miss Whitman," he whispered, easing down beside her, "I want your absolute and undivided attention."

Her breasts rose and fell quickly at the look in his eyes, at the sensations he was just beginning to arouse. "Nick, is loving you going to be enough?" she whispered. "I'm more than willing, but I know so little . . ."

"It doesn't matter," he murmured as his arms swallowed her, as his mouth burned down against hers in a kiss as slow and tender as it was passionate. "All you have to do," he added in a deep whisper, "is relax and do what

I tell you to. I'm going to show you all the slow, tender ways that a man expresses love. I'm going to be very gentle, and you're not going to be afraid of me. All right?"

Her arms looped around his neck and she felt with a sense of wonder his warm, hair-covered flesh melting down over her soft, bare body until she felt the brush of every fascinating inch of it. Her eyes widened and she gasped, her eyes telling him all that she felt. "Nick, I want to give you everything," she whispered, gasping under his hands, the satin brush of his hard mouth touching her in ways, in places, that she'd never dreamed of even in her most erotic fantasies. "Love me," she whispered, arching her body toward his mouth.

He chuckled softly, delightedly, as his hand reached over to turn out the light.

It was morning when she woke, to find herself looking up into patient, loving dark eyes with all the memories of the night before in them. Nicholas had been patient and tender, intent on giving pleasure as well as getting it. His expertise had quickly ignited Keena with a passion that bordered on anguish. She remembered opening her eyes at that instant and looking straight into his, amazed to find him watching her, his face taut with desire, his gaze fiercely loving as his powerful body over-whelmed hers.

"You . . . you watched me," she whispered shakily, still half-awake.

He bent and kissed her mouth tenderly, rev-erently. "I had to," he whispered. "It was beau-tiful. The moonlight, brighter than day on your face, those tiny, amazed little cries purr-ing out of you, your body trembling . . . I'll dream about it for the rest of our lives, Keena. You were exquisite."

Her fingers edged into his dark hair, where it was silver at the temples, tangling in its un-ruly thickness. "So were you," she whispered with a quiet smile. "Oh, Nick, I do love you so!"

He bent and kissed her open mouth roughly. "No less than I love you," he whis-pered. "How do you want to be married? In a church, with all the trimmings, or by a justice of the peace?"

"Any way at all," she murmured fervently.

"By a justice of the peace then," he replied, "because I want my ring on your finger as soon as possible."

"I won't change my mind," she assured him gently.

One corner of his mouth went up wickedly. "That isn't why."

Both her eyebrows went up as she searched his eyes.

He chuckled softly, smoothing a big hand across her flat stomach. "We've jumped the gun, honey."

She flushed delicately. "Afraid of wagging tongues?" she teased.

"Terrified of the stork," he whispered against her mouth. "I'm a respectable businessman, a pillar of the community . . ."

"A seducer of innocents," she whispered back, drawing his dark head down so that she could kiss him slowly.

"But you love me," he whispered with a broad grin.

"More than my own life. Even more," she laughed, "than my fabulous career."

"And now you have a whole new career," he murmured against her seeking mouth as he lowered his powerful body completely against hers.

"Hmmm?" she murmured breathlessly.

"Loving me," he replied, and her soft laughter was drowned out by the pressure of his smiling lips.